For more information, contact;

Beach Books Literature Publishing

P.O. Box 1658

La Mesa, CA, 91944

reedcandice@gmail.com

ISBN 13- 978-1545056127

The characters, places, incidents and situations in this book are imaginary and have no relation to any person.

Vixens of Vanishing Island

BY **CANDICE REED**

For Michelle Yale
Who would have laughed.
You are missed.

"Every murderer is probably somebody's old friend."

Agatha Christie

CAST OF CHARACTERS

Audrey Walsh—a TV reporter who is too smart for her own good—and everyone else's.

Cookie Armstrong—a former beauty queen who will do anything she can to stay young.

Tracy Morrow—a funny lady with a dark past.

Laverne White—she has the perfect husband—maybe a little too perfect.

Sandra Baxter—she was once married to God—but she divorced him.

Justine O'Keefe—she loves golf and women—in that order.

Jerdie Fields—a proud black woman whose twin sister embarrasses her—to death.

Jill Allen—her husband cheated on her with a stripper, but she got mad *and* even.

Belinda Rios—this chef cooks with jalapenos, but her kitchen gets even hotter when she is angry.

Mattie Friedman—she is an animal doctor who prefers dogs to people because they don't betray her.

Contents

CHAPTER ONE

———

OCT 10

I

"You look like you could use a Xanax," the flight attendant whispered to Audrey as she handed her a hot towel smelling of lavender and rosemary. Audrey realized that she was clenching her fists. As much as she tried to relax on the long flight, her jaw was so tight that she was grinding her teeth.

"Wow, is that a new perk of first class now?" she said, laughing a little as she sat up in the pod of her flying suite. "And yes, I desperately need a Xanax. Do you have any?"

The flight attendant was small and compact, with shiny black hair and equally sympathetic dark eyes. She had been Audrey's personal attendant for the entire trip. As soon as she came aboard, the flight attendant served Audrey champagne with two exquisite canapés—a caviar tartlet and a crostini with *salsa verde* and pickled fennel. The flight attendant even made up her bed while Audrey ate dinner and scribbled notes in a book.

"Hang on; I have one in my purse. You need to relax, Miss Walsh. We'll be landing in just a few hours and we want your experience with us to have been a good one. By the way, I love your show."

Audrey mouthed the word, "thanks," and turned her gaze out the jet's window. She could just make out the shadows of the Great Barrier Reef, but her mind drifted as she wondered if the reality show had been the right decision.

She reached into her bag and grabbed the printed itinerary for the tenth time on the flight, and perused the details of the *Vixens of Vanishing Island* reality series. After a moment, she grabbed her cell phone and checked the time—another two hours before landing. Great, she had time to wash her face, put on some makeup and change into her new Maggie London spring dress and wedge sandals. It was the perfect outfit, now that they had crossed the equator. She was quite happy to leave the New York autumn behind, since the weather had turned wet the last few days, with a possible hurricane headed straight for Manhattan. The season had always been a period of change for Audrey, and this fall was no exception. She didn't know what was on the other end of this transition. The only thing she did know was that she was on a plane headed for Sydney, and she might have some time to write; maybe even finish that memoir she started so long ago.

She was looking forward to the summer-like days of Australia and the sandy beaches where she could jump off the rocks for a snorkel. However, it was also a work trip. She had done in-depth research about the island—and the show—and would eventually put that information to good use. She had written down some facts: Vanishing Island belonged to a reclusive billionaire; there were sketchy rumors about how he made his money. She discovered that he rented the island to other rich people who valued their privacy, mainly because his wife was afraid of sharks and she wouldn't step foot on the tropical paradise he had spent millions on. He had turned the rock of brush, lizards and rodents into a heavenly retreat. It was only a few hours by boat from the Sydney Opera House. Audrey had left no stone unturned in her research, spending hours after work Googling the owner and taking notes on everything from the tides, to poisonous snakes, to shark attacks. She was a journalist, and she was damn good at her job. Word was that the owner wanted to sell and decided to loan the island to the reality production show as a way to feature his beautiful home—built on an 80-acre rock in the South Pacific. There was an airstrip, a helipad, and every room had a stocked bar—a few of the bathrooms even had wine coolers built under the vanity. She had seen that tidbit on the *Lifestyles of the Rich and Famous* back in the day. The for-sale of the compound had recently been featured in *People Magazine*, and *Vanity Fair,* which was a great PR move since there weren't many buyers of private islands in the Pacific Ocean walking around with a blank check. The gossip rags claimed that Johnny Depp was going to buy it, but she was sure Johnny already had his own island. And really, she reasoned, how many islands did one need?

Audrey had almost scored an interview with the *Pirates of the Caribbean* actor about a murder in the French village where he once lived, but then Missy St. James had snagged the interview for *TV Tonight!* Missy was a celebrity whore. Audrey, on the other hand, was a real television journalist and a former war reporter. She now hosted a show about true crime stories that aired on Friday nights. She mostly interviewed the husbands in prison who had killed their wives who always claimed they were innocent or the shifty best friend of the victim who was having an affair with the wife who put out a contract to kill her husband for the insurance money. Every now and then, though, she might like to interview someone about something normal. A movie star who had been married for 20 years or a new author whose first book was a bestseller would be a welcome change. Maybe an interview where she didn't have to run home and take a shower to cleanse the prison stench off her body. Oh well, she was semi-famous, made a ton of money and had a say in the producing of her show, *Inside Detective*. Life could be worse.

She opened her Chrome book and pulled up her emails, looking for the final one that detailed the information about the vixen show.

Dear Ms. Walsh; we look forward to seeing you on the evening of October 10 to begin filming the new reality series, "Vixens of Vanishing Island." You will be flown first-class to Sydney and then picked up at the Darling Harbour helipad for a 45-minute ride to the island. You will be joining nine other women journalists and TV personalities, along with Robert Close, the director and the rest of the crew. The show will follow the 'Vixens' as they talk about news and entertainment, partake in challenges and all things 'news.' It will be a smart, hip program highlighting the talents of professional newswomen. We are so glad you are on - board.

I will meet you on the island. Best, Ms. Owen.

She closed her computer as the flight attendant came around with a final call for mimosas. She placed her order as the woman pressed the Xanax into her hand. She glanced out the window again and knew that making this trip was the best decision of her life.

II

Cookie Armstrong couldn't believe Qantas Airlines had dumped her in business class for the 14-hour flight to Sydney from LAX. She normally flew business class and it was quite comfortable, but she figured that the producers of *Vixens of Vanishing Island* would spring for First Class. At least they didn't cheap out and place her in coach; if that had happened, she would have turned on her Jimmy Choos and walked off the show. When she received the offer to be part of the cast on the reality series, she told her husband, Kurt, that if the mansion on the island wasn't swankier than the Four Seasons in Santa Barbara, she would demand a raise. Her husband had already gone back and forth with the producers about her salary. They wanted to pay her scale since the show wasn't a done deal, but she told Kurt that she wanted NeNe Leakes money. At least Tamara Barney money, for God's sake! Kurt had exchanged dozens of emails with the head producer, Una-Nell Owen, over the salary, and they finally settled on a nice chunk of change. Kurt said Cookie could spend it any way she wanted. She'd already made a wish-list of designer clothes and a new purple Porsche, which she knew would set the tone for her role as a reality TV celebrity. If they wanted a vixen, Cookie announced to Kurt as they toasted her new adventure while dining at Bouchon, they were going to get a vixen!

Cookie fidgeted in her seat and pushed away the lunch of chicken schnitzel the flight attendant had served her earlier. She lightly touched her stomach. It was so flat she could hardly believe it. It made her deliriously happy. Dr. Hastings, the very best plastic surgeon in Santa Barbara, had assured her that she would be a size four after the liposuction and the tummy-tuck, but she had starved herself and run the beach from Stearns Pier to Goleta five days a week for the past month to make it down to a size one. She probably could have done it without the surgeon, but she didn't have the time.

Back in her pageant days, Cookie had transformed herself the summer she started trying out for Miss Suntan, but her father and her friends had conniption fits about her weight loss. Back then, she was super-anorexic and weighed 90 pounds. All she remembered about that summer was eating grapefruit. Nothing but grapefruit. Looking back, even though her mother pushed her to be in that first pageant, Cookie realized she wanted to win as much as her mother did. She desired to be pretty and perfect. If she won, then that would confirm her flawless figure and ideal weight, and it happened. Cookie won that first contest and she entered every pageant she could until the last pageant, which made her famous. Or infamous, she couldn't remember the right word. After that, she struggled with her weight and her confidence, even though she knew she was the hottest woman in her group of friends. The reality show was a way to get back that self-esteem, but if she was going to be on national television, it wasn't going to be as a size four, thank you very much. They said the camera added 10 pounds; now, at 5 feet 11 and 120 pounds and wearing size one, white, cropped 7 For All Mankind jeans, she was going to be the hottest vixen on the island. The other former beauty queens and their best friends that were appearing on the show would have a tough time receiving camera time when she strutted around in her tiny bikini. Her second facelift was holding up well. The Botox and Juvederm Dr. Hastings had injected last week left her 58-year-old face with a slightly puffy, dewy look. She only hoped the fake eyelashes that her esthetician applied yesterday would last. Her hair extensions were even more important, since there was no way she would be camera ready without them. She had inherited her mother's thin hair; when the wind blew, she had a small bald spot on the back of her head, so she had extensions put in every two weeks. Before she signed on to the show, she made sure the hair and makeup people were on board. The Owen woman assured her that the best makeup and hair stylists would be on set. *"It takes a village to get me looking like I do,"* she joked in her email to Una Owen. She wasn't kidding. She just hoped her friend Tracy had managed to lose a few pounds as she had instructed. She didn't want those other women judging her by her best friend—her only friend, if she thought about it—but that didn't bother her. Girlfriends were a pain in the ass. More than anything, pageants had shaped her relationships with women.

In the world of pageants, you might think someone was your friend, and then they would seek out a weakness and turn it around. Cookie never knew who she could trust. The other girls didn't like her; they spread rumors that were never true. She always wondered why they hated her—was it just because she was pretty, or was she actually not worthy of being liked? Even now, whenever she met somebody, she questioned whether they really liked her for herself, or if it was for her money and beauty. Sometimes being beautiful was such a chore.

Cookie peered out the window at the dark blue of the ocean. As she stared down, she made out the plane's shadow, surrounded by shimmering rings of color. It looked ghostly and made her cold. She realized she was shivering and felt an anxiety attack coming on. She snatched her purse from the floor and rummaged through it for her Prozac, found the bottle and shook out a pill. Cookie washed it down with her champagne and snapped the window-shade closed. She would be seeing enough of the water; quite honestly, she wasn't a fan. She told herself she was being ridiculous. It wasn't her fault that Heather Jackson (Miss Kansas 1981) had drowned while reenacting Houdini's water torture trick in the Miss America pageant. The horror on live TV broke all records as Heather pounded on the shatterproof glass trying to break out of the clear box. Just because she had asked Cookie to be the person to lock the box and Cookie had accidently snatched a real lock from the table didn't mean she was responsible for her death. It was an accident, the jury said. It was an accident, the judge said. Even though Heather and Cookie were roommates at the Hyatt Hotel did not mean she had access to the locks. Well, she did, but she would never play such a dirty trick on Miss Kansas just because she was taller, prettier and smarter than she was. Seriously, who crawls into a box of water as a talent anyway?

In the end, Cookie still didn't win. She took the runner-up prize, but she received some great parting gifts and was in the news more than the actual Miss America, with the trial and all. She ended up marrying her lawyer, Kurt Armstrong, and except for the occasional panic attacks around water, she had put the whole thing behind her.

Now, flying over the ocean and realizing she would be on an island, she couldn't help thinking about Heather staring at her in terror and pounding on the bulletproof glass. She would never forget the sight of Heather those last few moments as she glared at Cookie and mouthed the word 'bitch,' right before she died.

III

The helicopter ferrying Tracy Morrow was dipping up and down and freaking her out. The pilot was smiling and didn't seem worried, so she decided to take ten deep cleansing breaths, just as she did every night when she went on stage in Las Vegas. In and hold... and out. "Ohm," she hummed, figuring the pilot couldn't hear her. On her fourth exhale, his voice boomed in her headphones and she jumped in her seat.

"Your seat cushions can be used for flotation. In the event of an emergency water landing, please take them with our compliments," he said with a laugh.

"Jesus wept!" she yelled.

"She'll be right. Sorry about that, just making sure you're Ok," he said in his cute Aussie accent.

"Yes, I'm OK, funny guy," she giggled. "Hey, did you hear the joke about the blond who was taking helicopter lessons? The instructor said, "I'll radio you every 1000 feet to see how you're doing." At 1000 feet, the instructor radioed her and said she was doing great. At 2000 feet, he said she was doing well. Right before she got to 3,000 feet, the propeller stopped and she twirled to the ground. The instructor ran to where she crashed and pulled her out of the helicopter. He asked her, "What went wrong?" The blond said, "At 2,500 feet, I started to get cold, so I turned the big fan off."

"You're funny," her pilot said, laughing even louder.

"I better be," she said lighting up. "I'm a stand-up comic in Vegas. At the Rio. I've been there four years now."

"Wow, I think maybe I saw you once when I was on holiday in America," he said. "You look familiar. Do you know Joan Rivers?"

"She died," Tracy said.

"Oh yeah. How about Britney Spears? She lives in Vegas, right?"

Tracy had seen Britney a few times at the local Vons, after their shows were over, albeit, Brit played a larger room, but she had never spoken to her. Her friend Cookie called her a wimp all the time and urged her to talk to the star, but Tracy couldn't and wouldn't do it. Cookie was always bossing her around, telling her what she should do, who she should break up with, and who she should hang out with, not to mention her backhanded compliments.

"Wow, Trace, that dress doesn't make you look nearly as chubby as the dress you wore last time," she would say. Tracy didn't think she was a wimp other than with her BFF Cookie Armstrong, and had been since they had met in Hawaiian dance class when they were 12.

Tracy still questioned herself as to why they were still friends, since they had nothing in common anymore. Cookie had the easy life playing the perfect homemaker while Kurt, who was a former lawyer and now a sports agent, brought in millions of bucks. Tracy had worked her ass off in clubs all over the country for 20 years before landing at the Rio in the King's Lounge, where tickets averaged $72.55 and sat 150 people, and she was grateful. It was an awesome gig. She worked Monday through Thursday with three days off to be with her family—that is, she'd be with them if she *had* any family.

Tracy was almost 60 and had never married—her career was her life and the other comedians were her social circle. She spent the holidays with other entertainers and enjoyed it. She wished that just once Cookie would invite her to Christmas dinner at her huge home in the Santa Barbara hills. The house balanced over a canyon of eucalyptus trees with a view of the Pacific Ocean in the distance. Unfortunately, it wasn't likely to happen.

"I don't do Christmas dinner anymore," Cookie had recently told her on the phone. "I'm so over it. The kids don't care. They have their own lives, and I'm tired of cooking food for my mooching family to eat and not appreciate. Kurt and I will just kick back by the pool, drink Bloody Mary's and relax."

As if Cookie wasn't always kicking back by the pool drinking and relaxing. Tracy had no idea what her friend did with herself all day other than work out and take care of her face.

Speaking of relaxing, Tracy had looked forward to flying to Australia to be on an island for a month. She hadn't been sure at first. She didn't think she fit the 'vixen' mold, considering she lived in a condominium off the strip. She only used fillers in her face, and hardly ever wore makeup offstage, except for a little lipstick and mascara. Cookie was pushing her to have a mini-facelift, and had actually gone so far to make Tracy an appointment with Dr. Cohen in nearby Henderson, but she didn't keep the appointment. She didn't want a damn facelift, and she was going to tell Cookie to back-off on the subject when she saw her on the island. Well, maybe she would tell her, but in a nice way.

"Have you been to Australia before?" the pilot asked her.

"No, never, I don't travel much. If I go anywhere it's to visit a few friends in California. I did go to the Grand Canyon last year with a few showgirls and that was a blast. We caused quite a commotion. Four women topping out at six-feet, hiking in hot pants and midriff tops down into the canyon. Oh, and me of course, but nobody noticed me."

"I doubt that," the pilot said. "You're very pretty. I wish I had time to have Sunday arvo bevvies, but I'm snowed under."

Tracy wondered what the hell the pilot was saying, but then a small dot of land appeared and she forgot all about it. The pilot pushed and pulled on some levers, adjusted his headset and said, "Let's get you on the ground. You're the first one here, so you can really check out the place. I can't wait to tell everyone I met a famous stand-up comic."

Tracy smiled to herself. Maybe after being on this show, her life would change and someone would offer her parts on TV—maybe even a movie role. Life hadn't passed her by yet, she decided; this was a new beginning.

IV

"Gin and tonic," Laverne White called to the harried bartender.

"Make it a double for just a dollar more?"

"Sure, why not. I just have to get on a damn helicopter to fly to an island to be on a TV show with a bunch of old college gals from Nebraska, so I think a double is just what the doctor ordered," she said.

"Nebraska? Is that in America?" The bartender said over her shoulder as she grabbed a bottle of gin.

"Yes dear," Laverne smirked at the young woman who looked young enough to be her granddaughter as she set her drink and coaster on the bar in front of her. "It's in America."

She took a sip of her cocktail, and looked at the man sitting on the bar stool next to her.

"Holy smokes, what do they teach in the schools down here?" she asked him. "America is the greatest country on earth and people should know as much about it as their own, you see what I'm saying?"

She didn't wait for the man to answer.

"You know, I believe in America and I always thank the vets for our freedom. As Rush always says, 'when the people fear their government, that's tyranny, but when the government fears the people, there is freedom.' But what do Australians know? You're damn near socialists, which mean one step away from communism. Hoo, boy, I need to calm down or my blood pressure will go through the roof," she said as she took a slug of her drink. The man was watching the TV and didn't seem to be listening to her, but she continued.

"Goddamn, I love a good G and T. I love a good cigarette too but it seems the Aussies have the no smoking rule as well. Damn commies. I sure hope I can smoke on the island, but out of the camera's aim. If my honey Fred spots me with a Virginia Slims between my lips, he'll refuse to kiss me for a month. Fred is cute that way, but since I've been sneaking a ciggy twice a day throughout our 30-year-old marriage you would have thought he might have caught a whiff of smoke, but my Thera Breath drops work like a charm. The laser treatments for my lips every few years also keep my little secret safe."

She looked at her watch and glanced around. Over by the restrooms was a familiar face, but then she turned and her ass was rather wide so no, it couldn't be. Damn, the flight had made her a little ditsy. She'd only had four G and T's the whole flight from Dallas, but not much anything else. The reality show was making her a little nervous.

Laverne leaned closer to the man who wore cutoff jeans, a tank top and sandals and was invested in a segment about rugby on Sky News.

"I'm going to have a reunion with nine other gals from Beta Tau

Upsilon and I'm not so sure it's a good idea after all," she said. "Not a lot of those gals liked me much back then. They blamed me for some stupid thing that happened during my senior year when I was head Pooh-Bah of BTU. I'll admit some of the hazing got out of hand. That fat little freshman freaked out and told the school authorities, and we were shut down the following year. But come on, hazing was something everyone did back then. Christ on a cracker, I heard recently about some frat hazing that led to someone dying. At least that didn't happen when I was in charge. Nobody had to know about our little issue until Mary Kaye Valentine, who was pledging, spilled the beans. She told the Dean that I ordered the pledges to be taken to the Willow Bowl, where we forced them to crawl through the mud while we screamed and spit on them, which might be close to the truth."

Laverne looked down at her hands, covered in diamond rings, and thought about that night. The hazing committee decided that the pledges should stand in a pool of water that the sorority members had peed in. Later, they were forced to sit naked on a washing machine while any body part that jiggled was circled with a Sharpie pen. The next day they were blindfolded, and forced to chug a vile alcoholic punch while shooting vodka shots. That's when Mary Kaye lost consciousness. They had to call an ambulance for her, the lightweight. Besides the alcohol poisoning, she had bruises and cuts all over her body and her front tooth was broken. She claimed that she was one step from dying. Laverne thought that was a bit dramatic, and that maybe Miss Valentine couldn't hold her liquor.

Oh well, she had graduated early—seeing as she was a little bit pregnant with Fred's baby—and left in the middle of the night; she didn't even say goodbye. She was damn nervous about seeing those girls again. Ms. Owen, the producer, had assured her that her Greek sisters were excited to see her. She said even Mary Kaye, who had

15

several operations to cover her scars, had forgiven her. As if Miss Valentine shouldn't share some of the blame, being that she was too overweight to have even tried out for B.T.U. in the first place. Whatever, Laverne shrugged to herself. She had a helicopter to catch.

"Nice talking to you," she said to her seatmate. She stood up, pulled her Chico's palazzo pants out of her butt, adjusted her kimono-sleeved top and grabbed her carry-on. She tossed down the last of her drink, plunked 50 cents on the counter and ran toward the exit.

V

In a cab, Sandra Baxter sat upright as she did at mass every Sunday and on all holy days as well. She was only 40, but people often mentioned that she was an old soul. It had to do with the training she'd had when she became a nun with the sisters of Our Lady of the Weeping Virgin. "Stand up straight, don't speak unless spoken to and don't mollycoddle anyone," they would nag over, and over. She had loved the whole idea of being a nun—mainly because she liked being superior to people—but when she finally took her vows she realized that she hated the whole gig. She had no interest in feeding the homeless or praying for other people, she just wanted to have a nice quiet home and not be around needy people like her eight siblings.

Sandra's family was devoutly religious. They attended Mass on Sunday and ate Gorton's Fish Sticks on Friday, just like all the other Catholics she knew. In high school, she began to think about being a nun and became obsessed with religion. She wrote about religious topics for almost every assignment—even her science papers. When she was a junior, she asked her father if she could follow her vocation, but he needed her at home to help with her siblings, and told her to wait until after college. She was secretly thrilled when her parish priest informed her father that if she "lost" her vocation because she waited to follow God's call, they would all go to hell. Her father helped her pack her bags the first day of summer, and she began her religious life in earnest.

The culture shock almost killed her. She lived with 30 girls; they slept, worked, and studied together. She knew that she and the others should have been learning to dress, to use makeup, to carry purses, to notice boys and to become women, but the nuns made sure to smother their natural instincts. They wore identical uniforms, were makeup free, and were forced to focus their attention on God and Jesus and how to please them. They were to be Brides of Christ, and all their love and attention was to be directed heavenwards.

When it was time to take her final vows she was plagued with doubts. Mother Superior told her it was a test from God, or maybe even a temptation from the devil. She knew deep in her heart of hearts it was the ugly habit she was forced to wear, and the rules against makeup. Yes, she was that shallow, and she had made her peace with it. She left the nunnery when she was 24 with a grocery bag filled with her few belongings and went straight to Macy's, where she found a job at the MAC counter. They hired her at first sight because of her beautiful skin.

Sandra was an attractive woman, with her dad's red hair and her mother's beautiful teeth. The fact was, though, she rarely smiled. Oh, she used to laugh sometimes when she gathered with a group of girlfriend's a few years after she left the nunnery, but even that turned bad. Things were said, and feelings were hurt, as if she actually cared. She just went for the wine, the social connections and to sell the makeup line she created after learning everything she could from the gay boys who worked at MAC alongside her—even though she disapproved of their lifestyle.

Those boys used to tease her that she was an old lady, because of the stern looks she gave customers who disagreed with her or how stuck-up she acted. After a while, the boys taught her how to dress her age, and how to do her hair. She was a natural makeup artist and she sometimes—begrudgingly—did the boys' makeup when they were headed to a nightclub.

She thought back on those days and gave a little thanks to the Virgin Mary that the homosexuals had given her fashion tips, although she would never say it aloud. Now, being chauffeured through the streets of Sydney, she held her hands in her lap and admired her clothing choices as the driver honked at pedestrians. She was wearing a short Stella McCarthy floral short-sleeve dress with pink heels, and tasteful jewelry including a small 18-carat cross. It was quite pleasant in Sydney this time of year, with the gorgeous Jacaranda trees and their purple blooms. She almost enjoyed her cab ride to the harbor where she would be catching a helicopter to Vanishing Island. She was there to provide her makeup line and consult for the new reality show about vixens. What a ridiculous name. Who would want to be called a vixen anyway? Sandra knew two definitions of 'vixen;' a fox and a spiteful woman. She had never even seen a fox outside of the zoo, but she had known quite a few spiteful bitches in her life. She set her lips closely, thought about some of those women and shuddered. They turned out to be meaner than the nuns. She thought of something pleasant to wipe the memories of the women from her mind. She closed her eyes and reflected on the new line of creamy eye shadows she had recently created that came in a dozen colors from her favorite ice cream flavors. They were yummy; she had invented a little spoon to apply the shadow to the eyes. The Internet was already going crazy for the release. That made her smile. She opened her eyes. The back of her driver's head greeted her. She frowned and wondered if all cab drivers around the world were immigrants. At least this one didn't try to have a conversation with her because as usual, she would ignore him. Now

19

that she thought about it, she was quite anxious to get to the heliport. She mentally re-read the email, which she had memorized.

Dear Ms. Grayson,

I hope you remember me—we met at the Beauty Expo USA show in Los Angeles last year.

We are premiering a new reality TV show called Vixens of Vanishing Island, filmed off the coast of Sydney, Australia, and we are looking for a new makeup line that we can also advertise as the 'Makeup of the Vixens.' Your product impressed me so much—I do hope you take me up on the offer to come to the island to consult with our make-up artists and the cast. I think it will benefit your business, and you might even get a cameo on the show!

We will whisk you across the water in a helicopter and put you up in one of the private Balinese-style villas crowning a hill above the beach. You will experience all the luxuries that the cast will enjoy and your product line, 'Hell's Angels' will be famous!

Looking forward to seeing you again, U.N.O-

What was that name? She let her mind rewind to all the people she met at the show. She couldn't quite place this person, but what the heck. If the show turned out to be a bust, she would at least get a nice vacation out of the deal. On a private island—which was a plus. If only she could remember this Uno person. Oh well, she would find out soon enough.

VI

"I hope their golf course is better than the last course I played in Australia," Justine O'Keefe said aloud as she searched for the greens from her seat in the helicopter. "It's that course up in Brisbane, where six man-eating bull sharks live in the lake on the 14th tee, do you know it?" The pilot didn't answer and she shrugged. "Personally, I thought it was a stupid stunt. I was just there to play golf. The course was average, but there were some challenging holes with a nice balance of bunkers, trees and water. The fairways were well kept, but the greens were extremely fast, which made missing the hole sometimes a punishing two putts back. The only downside to a great day of golf, were the tee-off areas that were kind of rough and not level, and the sharks, which gave a new meaning to water hazards." She let out a loud laugh, but the pilot was concentrating on his landing. "I like to play alone. I don't want some other broad to be chattering away about her kids or her animals. Golf is my job and my hobby. Nothing else really matters to me." She gazed out the window again, twisting her neck from side to side. "Where the hell is the course on this damn island?"

Oh well, she would find it as soon as she changed her shoes and grabbed a Gatorade. Hopefully she didn't have to have some meet and greet crap until after she got in 18 holes. She could care less about talking to anyone, but she supposed she should take a few minutes and play nice to the manager—Una, Uno or something like that—who was footing the bill for her flight and stay. Not to mention paying her to teach some gals how to play golf. That wasn't a vacation as far as she was concerned. Most women played golf to drink and gossip, which she had no time for these days. She struggled to pay her rent as golf pro at her father's course back in Los Angeles. She started working there after that thing happened when she played the Dinah Shore a decade ago. The last time she had golfed with other women for 'fun,' she was roped into hanging out with them for a few years, then all hell broke loose. Women for the most part were bitches, which was hard on her love life, considering she loved the damn bitches so much.

Justine stretched her muscular, tan legs, pulled down the leg of her lime green golf shorts, and checked for crumbs on her paisley polo shirt. She examined herself in her compact and decided that her bleached blond bob was perfect, as were the multitude of freckles that dotted her still-cute tan face. She ignored the deep crow's feet sprouting from the corners of her eyes, snapped the mirror shut and braced for the landing.

VII

Jerdie Fields locked her adorable flat in Brighton, a suburb of Sydney, and walked downstairs to her car. The white sands of Brighton Beach were right across the street, and her flat looked out onto historic Botany Bay, but she was still excited to fly to Vanishing Island to star on a reality show. As usual, she would probably be the only African-American in the bunch, but she planned to make the most of it. She was tall and beautiful and held herself like the queen her daddy always said she was, even though it took some time for her to realize it. Her skin was a pretty mocha color and her eyes a deep-set brown. Her hair—her crowning glory—was a natural afro, which stopped many people in the streets. She only wore designer clothes, and didn't need Botox or fillers even at 42, and she was proud of that fact.

"Black don't crack," her nana would say. Jerdie would roll her eyes, but it was true. But that didn't mean she didn't take care of her mind, body and soul. Her business was in the health industry, and it had made her quite wealthy.

The producer had informed her via email that the show was about self-made businesswomen. Even though she originally acquired the seed money to start her vitamin company, 'Sun Sisters,' from her ex-husband, she considered herself self-made. Apparently, so did the producers.

Beautiful and successful, yes that's me exactly, she thought.

She had moved to Sydney a few years earlier to open another office. Jerdie loved it so much that she decided to move the entire company from Chicago to Australia. She had to lay off almost her whole staff, but that was the price of business.

Her nana tried to guilt-trip her into moving back to the US, but she wasn't having any part of it. She loved Sydney and almost loved being an African-American in this country. Almost because racism was a thing in Australia just like the States, but she wasn't afraid of the cops in Sydney like some of her relatives were back home. Of course, her sister Birdie had plenty to be afraid of in regards to the cops, being that she was homeless and a drug addict.

"You have to come back and find Birdie," Nana emailed her just about every week.

She ignored the plea. There were professionals that were equipped to handle addicts and it wasn't her job anymore. She wasn't her sister's keeper, even if she was her twin. Birdie's addictions took up all of the air in the room, leaving no space for her to talk about her own life challenges to her nana.

"Birdie ruined our family," she said quietly to herself. "She's the star of the show and everyone else is left behind."

Her sister had been to rehab countless times; even jail once or twice. She had heard that Birdie had a prison sentence hanging over her head, but she didn't want to think about it. The last time they had all been together, Jerdie had found needles and spoons in her sister's backpack. She told her nana, who freaked out and Birdie manipulated her into believing it was the only way for her to take her methadone. She made Jerdie out to be the bad guy, and that was the last time she had ever tried to help. Her sister made her own choices—the one to smoke meth was her worst.

Some people blamed Jerdie for Birdie's problems but she wasn't buying into it. She felt as if people who knew them only had room for her sister's baggage, so she became the independent twin. Byron had married *her*, not her sister. And then Jerdie had divorced him. Birdie shouldn't have let it get to her. Jesus, he was just a guy. Birdie had been just as beautiful as Jerdie—maybe more so—but not anymore. Birdie had married drugs and it had given her missing teeth, a bone-thin body and scabs on her face. Maybe if she had been a little tougher and less thin-skinned she could have moved on and found someone else.

"Apparently, I grabbed all the backbone in the womb," Jerdie said aloud as she started her Mercedes and drove toward Darling Harbour.

VIII

Jill Allen climbed up the front steps of the island retreat dressed in a blue-checked button front shirtdress and white sandals from Chadwick's of Boston, the only store she bought her clothes from other than EBay. She gazed over at the Bali Hi House, with its wraparound terrace filled with hammocks, sofas and vibrant rugs in reds and oranges and throw pillows bursting with colorful flower prints. She could see a fully stocked bar past the dining area, but had been told by the pilot to walk straight to her room. She sighed heavily and pulled her bag in the direction of what appeared to be a hand-carved Balinese staircase, if she wasn't mistaken. As she bumped her bag to the top, she was still fuming that she had had to hand her cell phone over to her pilot, but at least she was able to keep her laptop.

She glanced up at the ceiling and thought that the thatched roof was a little obvious, having once stayed at the Brando in Tahiti a decade earlier. When she walked into her room, she tried not to be impressed, but the French doors were open to a 180-degree view of the island and the surrounding ocean, and there were two other terraces connected to her room. She made the rounds of her large suite. It had a hot tub just inside the doors and a flat screen TV built into the bed, which was made of teakwood with a silk palm frond canopy.

"OK, this is pretty nice," she said out loud, not knowing if the cameras were already rolling.

Jill spied a slightly smaller bar than what she had seen downstairs in the corner of her room and almost sprinted to the wine refrigerator. Inspecting the array of bottles, she found one she liked, grabbed an opener and poured a full glass of 2013 Rombauer Carneros Chardonnay. She sank down on a big chair filled with purple and blue silk pillows and regarded the ocean. Waves crashed violently on the rocks below. A flock of large birds flew through clouds that were threatening to turn dark, but it didn't matter. This was going to be interesting, this whole TV series thing, she thought; she hoped it would be good. She needed a little change of scenery since her ugly and public divorce and trial five years earlier. She was almost excited to be on a reality program, although she knew that, at the age of 62, she was going to be the oldest woman on the show. Maybe she could make a friend, something she was lacking. She used to have so many friends some of them so close she could tell them her secrets—but in the end, they had abandoned and betrayed her. Just as Henry had done. She took a big gulp of wine to erase the painful memory. Jill swallowed more chardonnay, then, took a deep breath. She gazed across the room at the mirror and was happy to see that, at a distance, her scars from her third—no wait, her fourth—facelift were invisible. All thanks to her plastic surgeon in Mexico, who cost less and did better work that her former doctor in La Jolla. She had gained a little weight in the past year, and she realized that even though she was wearing two pairs of Spanx, she still had a stomach bulge. She sighed. Going under the knife for her face was one thing, but she wasn't so vain that she was going to have them cut into her stomach too. There had to be some sort of endpoint when it came to plastic surgery, although she had some former friends who had every bump and lump sucked and cut out. Oh well, at least she wasn't as insecure as those people. After another sip, she spotted a handwritten note sitting on the bamboo coffee table, so she stood and walked toward it. Damn, her knees hurt like hell. Too many years skiing on the slopes of Aspen. She was getting old fast, she noted, as she slipped her reading glasses on her face.

"Dear Ms. Allen:

We hope you will enjoy the finest accommodations found anywhere on earth. Your bar is stocked with your favorite beverages and there is a small kitchen where you can prepare some of your favorite foods between meals. Dinner will be served at the Bali Hi House tonight in the Great Room at 5pm, starting with a cocktail hour. Please stay in your room until we call you to join the other women starring on the show. We know you will be excited and surprised by the other stars. We want you to have fun and be yourself during the filming.

Thank you for coming, Una.

IX

"*Ay, dios mio,*" said Belinda Rios after she read the letter she found on the table in her luxurious room. '*Dinner at 5p.m. starting with cocktails. Stay and enjoy your room until then…*' hell, she could stay here forever, looking at the ocean view from her outdoor tub.

Belinda had stayed in some swanky places, but for a girl growing up in Santa Rosa, California, and raised in a grape picker's shack, this was the ultimate hotel. She prayed the show would be renewed for 10 seasons like that Orange County series. Even though she owned three successful restaurants in Napa and Los Angeles, it didn't have to end there. She was convinced she was supposed to be the sassy Latina vixen on this show, and she was ready for it. She wasn't the least bit ghetto, but she could bring the spice and be the *chica del barrio* if it got her more screen time. Belinda loved her career, but she loved being famous even more. When the LA Times featured her on the front of the food section five years ago, she framed the article and sent copies to all of her family members in her Christmas card. She wasn't the least bit humble. In fact, she felt being humble was a waste of time. If she wasn't going to sing her own praises, who would?

Belinda stretched her arms, stood up and stepped out of the tub.

Her large breasts didn't quite match the rest of her body, but she had paid a small fortune for them and she made sure to wear clothes that showed them off. She was a bit bowlegged, but her boobs distracted from her legs, so she didn't care. She had extensions in her long straight black hair. Even though she was only 39, she had already had her eyes done and made sure she brought her own Botox to the island. Her sister was a nurse and had given her a small bag of syringes filled with Botox, warning her to keep them cool and to have someone help her with the shots, but Belinda knew how to inject herself; she had a past.

She stood naked and looked through the bar. She found a bottle of Meyer's rum, fresh pineapple juice and mixed herself a drink. She padded to the balcony and plunked her naked rear on a teakwood chair with a soft, cashmere cushion. She couldn't wait for the show to start. Not only was she going to be the best vixen on this *chingada* island, she was going to be a star.

X

Mattie Friedman perused the cocktail dresses provided by the producer in the closet of her beautiful suite and tried to pick the perfect one for her meeting with the other women. She wasn't a classic beauty, but she knew that she made up for it with chutzpah. She worked long shifts and rode her bike 10 miles to and from work, rain or shine. Her brown curly hair was shoulder length; she made sure she had time for highlights and a cut every two months. Mattie was a size 8, down 20 pounds since receiving her invitation to the island. She was extremely tan since she was outdoors much of the time, ministering to her larger patients. She had only brought one suitcase, since clothes weren't really an issue in her line of work and she couldn't wear her colorful scrubs. Well, she could, and she did on many of her days off, but she certainly wasn't going to go on TV looking like a schlep. She bought some great clothes at the Jewish Council Thrift Store near her house, including the Jaclyn Smith Women's Tiered Tank Top she was wearing, paired with NYDJ Dayla Cuffed Cropped Jeans with tummy control and hot pink platform shoes from Kohl's. She felt good about her wardrobe, but the cocktail dresses were appreciated. She tried to decide on the best one for the meet and greet.

She didn't really have the full picture of what was going on, but she could guess. The check for $50,000 and the letter from the producer of the Vixens of Vanishing Island had given Mattie the gumption to tell her boss at the Pooch N' Puss Animal Hospital that she was taking some time off for the first time in five years. Of course, it was never a vacation when you were a veterinarian and you were within house call distance. The producer had wanted someone with medical training and the doctor she had hired came down with some weird disease. Someone gave her Mattie's name. Obviously she wasn't a people doctor, but the producer said she just wanted someone who could perform CPR and administer some first aid if needed. Since they were on an island in the Pacific Ocean with 10 women—some in menopause, some not in tip-top shape—there were going to be meds dispensed and nerves soothed with a little TLC and valium. For $50,000 and an island vacation, Mattie could do that. Besides, medicine was mostly faith healing anyway. She had a good bedside manner—people respected her profession, and animals loved her. Most people liked her as well, except her boss and a few former friends. She was trying not to think about why Dr. Corbett was always on her ass about the amount of time she spent on the animals when her alarm went off. It was 4pm: time to start dressing and go downstairs to meet the vixens.

CHAPTER TWO

————

I

Cookie finished flat ironing her long blond hair, careful not to leave the heat on her extensions. She admired herself in the mirror and adjusted her boobs a few times in her Herve Leger strapless foil bandage dress. She wanted to buy a size 0, but Libby—her personal shopper at Nordstrom's—insisted that her breasts were too big for that particular size. Cookie hadn't believed her. When she finally stuffed herself into the damn thing in the dressing room, she almost fainted from the pressure and started to wheeze. Libby heard her and helped her out of the dress without ripping it, which was helpful because she certainly didn't need to buy two $1,300 dresses. Actually, the producer told her she wouldn't have to buy any dresses for the show, but she wasn't going to trust the wardrobe person without going over her demands: lots of cleavage, form fitting, no pinks or pastels and at least three-inch heels, so she would be over six feet tall. Time most likely took its toll on the other pageant girls—although some might have gone the same plastic surgery route as she did—but if she were taller than they were, she would look like the winner she was supposed to be.

Cookie glanced at the clock on her bedside table and realized she had ten more minutes before going to the Great Room to begin the series. She applied her Chanel lipstick no. 44 —aptly named La Vixen—and smiled wide and fake.

"Oh Jessica, you look fantastic for your age," she practiced in the mirror and then laughed. "Actually, you look like shit, but that's a nice dress."

Cookie turned and walked restlessly around the room, decorated perfectly in soft sandy beige and crème with off-white rugs on the teak floor. There were plenty of mirrors so that she could see herself everywhere she looked. Her bed was low, but the mattress was soft and covered with a turquoise blue bedspread that matched the sparkling ocean, which she could see as she sat on her bed. She moved over to the white fireplace and picked up the lone object on the mantel. It was a small cheap frame with a poem in it, which, she thought, didn't go with the room at all. She decided to read it to waste the last few minutes before she would make her entrance.

Ten little vixens went out to drink wine;
One choked her little self and then there were nine.
Nine little vixens gossiped until late;
One overslept herself and then there were eight.
Eight little vixens having a spa day in heaven;
One said she'd stay there and then there were seven.
Seven little vixens chopping up their trail mix;
One chopped herself in half and then there were six.

Six little vixens trying to stay alive;
A needle pricked one and then there were five.
Five little vixens wearing Michael Kors;
One stopped ticking and then there were four.
Four little vixens floating on the sea;
A shark swallowed one and then there were three.
Three little vixens relaxing by the pool;
One got stoned and then there were two.
Two little vixens running in the sun;
One was burned up and then there was one.
One little vixen left all alone;

She went and hanged herself….and then there were none.

"Well that was depressing, and it barely rhymes," Cookie said. She placed the framed poem back on the mantel. She marched across the room and looked out her open French doors to the vast expanse of ocean glistening in the evening sun. The water was so peaceful. *Water…so calm yet dangerous. Drowning…gasping for breath…drowning… clawing…fighting for her life…drowned…*

"Stop," she reprimanded herself. No, she wouldn't remember… she would stop thinking about it. All of that was over…

II

Audrey was tired. She drained the last of her Red Bull and vodka as she stood on the deck, looking out at the sea. Her eyeballs ached. Damn, she hoped she didn't look as tired as she felt. She had recently cut her shoulder-length hair to a short, sexy bob. Her colorist had applied a light brown base with some baby-blond highlights focused on the ends. Her wide green eyes were rimmed with dark eyeliner, and she wore a nude lipstick to go with her golden tan. She didn't think anyone would notice her exhaustion.

She hadn't always been so put together. When she had been a war correspondent, she wore khakis, T-shirts and hiking boots; her unruly curls were tied back in a haphazard ponytail. Now, her closet was filled with her own collection of classic luxury designers, like Valentino, Carolina Herrera, and Ralph Lauren, along with some fun pieces by Lilly Pulitzer and a few other whimsical designers. It was great to be able to wear beautiful clothes for her job, but she did miss the adrenalin of reporting on real-time news.

Audrey had started in journalism because she wanted to make a difference. She aspired to change the world. She wanted to right the injustices that she saw, so she took baby steps at the beginning. She started as a features writer on a very small newspaper called the *Daily*

Sun in her hometown of San Luis Obispo, California, where she covered everything from ugly-dog contests to local town council meetings. From there she worked her way up to the *Los Angeles Times*, where she worked as a war correspondent when the California newspaper was the center of journalism. Every journalist would have killed their grandmother to get that gig.

She reported on the 7/7 bombings in London in 2005, and quickly realized what a rush it was to be running against the tide—which is what journalists do if they're doing their job—sprinting down Tavistock Square after bomb had gone off on a double-decker bus and everybody else was scurrying in the other direction. She also realized that she was slightly crazy at the time, and thought maybe she should be more cautious in her approach to protect herself.

Audrey wiped a small tear away thinking back on her career decisions.

"Pull it together, Walsh," she said quietly.

She cursed herself for forgetting to bring her Adderall, which she took even though she didn't have ADD. She was always tired these days, but that's the way it was. This was her first time away from her show for more than a few days, but it would be worth it.

"Everything changes tonight," she whispered.

Audrey smoothed down her black Michael Kors lace sheath dress, smiled to herself and walked downstairs. She was still smiling when a bell rang, a door opened automatically and she walked through it.

CHAPTER THREE

———

I

The only woman Laverne saw as she walked into the Great Room was the Latin girl, Belinda, and she immediately knew it was a setup. She turned, but the door shut behind her. She started to swear. Then she remembered they were recording the show and her contract stated that she had no right to edit her reaction, so she held her tongue and walked into the room smiling wide.

"Belinda, how nice to see you. You're all grown up," she said through gritted teeth as she went in for a hug.

"Demonios!"

Laverne was confused. "Why are you speaking Mexican?" she asked. "You never did before."

Belinda rolled her eyes. "Hello Laverne, it's nice to see you. I guess. What are you doing here? Aren't you too old to be a vixen?"

"Honey, I was born a vixen," Laverne said making her way to the bar. "Are we the only two here?"

"So far," replied Belinda. "Who the hell knows who'll walk through the door next? What did they tell you about the show?"

"It was supposed to be about my old sorority sisters, but I'm kind of relieved," she said pouring some Tanqueray over a small amount of tonic. "They really didn't like me that much. How about you? What's the story?"

"*Hot Vixens of the Restaurant World*," she said.

"Oh that's right, I heard you own a taco shop."

Belinda stared at her in amazement. "I own a tapas and sangria bar. Actually, I own three. One in Santa Monica, another in Newport Beach and a third one in Napa."

"Well, excuse me," Laverne said taking a large sip of her drink.

"*Por Dios.*"

"Hey, cut that out and speak English."

"I can speak any way I want. You don't get to boss me around like you used to do. That was eight years ago and I'm a different person. Meanwhile, you seem to be the same old Laverne. Only, you know, older."

"Listen here missy…" Laverne started to say. Suddenly, two teak doors slid open simultaneously and they both turned to greet the next vixen.

II

Jerdie and Jill walked into the room at the same time, but they had different reactions.

"Goddammit," Jerdie said. Her eyes darted around the room at her former friends, a shadow of a scowl on her beautiful face.

"Oh, hi Jerdie," Jill said. "Well this is a surprise. Laverne, you look good. Long time no see, Belinda."

Belinda rolled her eyes again. Laverne took the last sip of her drink and looked over at the bar.

"What kind of joke is this?" Jerdie asked. "I've been tricked. I want to talk to the producer." She looked around for a camera. "Hello? Is anybody watching? This is not what I signed up for. I need a phone to get out of here. I don't like these women. I can only imagine…"

The doors opened again and out walked Mattie and Justine, both dressed in navy blue matching Zac Posen off-the-shoulder silk sheath dresses.

"Well this is awkward," Mattie said slowly as she surveyed the room. "And by awkward, I don't mean my dress selection."

41

Candice Reed

Justine walked toward Jerdie and gave her a quick hug. "Hey there girl, long time no see."

Jerdie didn't hug back and Justine stepped away.

"Jesus, I'm not hitting on you. Relax already. I'm just trying to be friendly. You know, like old times? When we were friends. When we were all friends?"

"We're not friends, we're strangers with memories," Jerdie said. "We were different people with different lives. Walking away from the group…"

"The group had a name," chuckled Laverne. "Remember what we called ourselves?"

"Ladies who Lunch!" said Belinda and Jill at the same time. Jill smiled sadly.

"Woo-hoo!" yelled Laverne. No one else joined her. "Fine, be that way. But hey, we had some fun times."

"Until we didn't," Mattie said. "When the first in the group walked away it went downhill from there."

"Oh please, she thought she was better than the rest of us," Laverne said. "And she was a liberal."

"Yes, there was that," Jerdie said. "Always thought she had the answers. Always throwing her knowledge of politics and name-dropping in our face in that passive-aggressive way. Damn, it got on my nerves. Oh shit, I wonder if she's on the show too."

"Oh my God, what if everyone is on the show?" Belinda said.

"This could get ugly."

Mattie chuckled. "I think that's what the producer had in mind. Damn, I wonder how she knew about us. It's not like we're famous."

"Some of us are," Belinda said.

Jerdie snorted.

"What? My restaurants are famous. I've been in the papers, and *Bon Appetite* even ran a tiny review about my place in Napa. You're just jealous because you sell vitamins, Jerdie. Don't you sell a vitamin that makes you less of a bitch?"

Jerdie took a step closer to Belinda. She was a head taller than the younger woman, but Belinda didn't blink. Jerdie looked her over, taking in her in; Belinda wasn't dressed like the others. Instead, she went for monochrome chic in a sleeveless white blouse with a triangular cut- out revealing her cleavage, trendy wide-legged trousers and black high-heeled sandals.

Her dark hair cascaded in gentle waves over her shoulders and it covered up one of her eyes as she struck a defiant pose. She looked great, being the youngest in the room, but Jerdie wasn't buying it.

"I keep it real *chica*, and that's a promise," Belinda continued. "I may be a *perra*, but at least I'm honest."

"And now you're calling me a liar about what?" Jerdie asked.

"Oh, you remember," Belinda said, turning her back on her former friend.

"Ladies, we just got here, nobody is calling anyone a liar," Jill said.

Belinda shot her a dirty look. "Seriously, Jill?"

The discussion was interrupted by the doors once again opening, and both Jill and Laverne let out a whoosh of relief.

III

"Here she comes," Cookie sang as Tracy stepped quickly to follow her friend. "Almost Miss America...oh no! No, I did not come 8,000 miles for this!"

Tracy surveyed the room and smiled. "Oh goodness, Jill and Laverne, it's so nice to see you again. How crazy is this? A show about vixens and that pretty much describes us. This is great. Don't you think this will be fun Cookie?"

"If you could shut the hell up that would be just lovely," Cookie said sternly, her long legs carrying her into the middle of the Great Room. "This sucks. I thought it was going to be about beautiful former pageant contestants, only—you know—older."

"As usual you haven't aged Cookie," Justine said. "Just don't stand too close to the window, you might melt."

Cookie ignored the barb and she ignored Justine. That's what she would do, she thought. Ignore everyone but Tracy. And, maybe Mattie. Mattie was OK, but was slightly crazy and nobody could understand what she said most of the time anyway. On second thought, she wouldn't ignore them. She would antagonize them and boss them around, just like the old days. That would make her the villain of the

45

show, which would give her the most airtime. Everyone loved the biggest mean girl on these types of shows. Hell, she would just act natural. That was the plan. But wait, she scanned the room. A door opened and everyone held their breath as Sandra Baxter regally walked in. She judged the group of women, just as quickly dismissed them, blessed herself and headed straight to the bar.

IV

"So Sandy, how've you been?" Laverne asked, a fresh gin and tonic in her hand. "Are ya single or are you still married to God?"

"It's Sandra, Laverne, and I haven't been a nun for more than a decade, as you well know."

"Oh sorree," Laverne said, throwing up her hands, some of her drink sloshing onto the floor. "I'm a Protestant, what do I know about Catholics?"

Sandra took a delicate sip of her white wine and gave the older woman a look she had gleaned from Mother Superior. "Other than making sure you know about other people's business, what else do you know Laverne?"

"Excuse me?"

"Hey," said Tracy, walking in between the two women. "Did you hear? Mother Superior at the Convent of St. Agnes got all of the nuns together for a little meeting. She said, "Sisters, we've discovered a case of syphilis in the house!" Whereupon little sister Mary Catherine clasped her hands together, fell to her knees and exclaimed,"Oh, thank the Lord! We've all been getting so tired of chardonnay!"

Jerdie laughed aloud, a few of the women snickered, but Sandra shot a laser beam of hatred toward the comic.

"Wow, tough crowd," Tracy said under her breath. "I was just trying to diffuse the situation."

"Oh my God," Cookie cackled. "That was so inappropriate yet so funny."

Tracy brightened. "Thanks Cookie."

Cookie flipped her hair with her hand and strode over to the former nun.

"So who have you been judging these past eight years, Sandra? You still holding on to that vow of chastity? Oh wait, I remember, weren't you selling Avon or Mary Kay or something?"

Sandra glared at Cookie, taking in her face and her newly sculpted body squeezed into her designer dress, and then spoke.

"Fake nails, fake hair, and fake smile. Bitch, are you sure you weren't made in China?"

The other women fell over themselves laughing as Cookie stood there, her mouth open in shock.

V

As the door opened, Audrey heard the laughter of women and thought, this won't be so bad. She stepped into the room and the amusement stopped. She was stunned to see familiar faces, trying to remember how they used to look before all the plastic surgery, their bad hairstyles, and their fashion faux pas. She almost smiled fondly, until she realized nine pairs of eyes were staring at her with different degrees of hate.

Oh no. She had misjudged the situation, but it was too late now. Everything was in motion. She couldn't back out, even if she wanted to. Until the show was over, they were all stuck on Vanishing Island.

CHAPTER FOUR

———

I

"I can't believe you have the nerve to be here," Cookie said, walking toward Audrey at a fast clip, considering the height of her heels. "Who invited you?"

"Who invited *you*?" Audrey replied, turning her back on Cookie. "Hi Belinda, how've you been? I love your restaurants. I went to one with my boyfriend, the one in Santa Monica. The *Gambas al Ajilloy* were to die for, kudos to your success."

Belinda looked nervously around the room. "Uh, thanks. Whatever."

Audrey laughed. "Afraid to talk to me? Wow, what are you afraid of, the wrath of Cookie? She can't hurt you. You're a successful business woman."

"I'm not afraid of anyone, especially you," Belinda said. "You tried to hurt me. You tried to hurt all of us, but it didn't work. We stayed friends without you."

Audrey looked around the room and observed the body language of the women. Some had turned their backs on her, others crossed their arms in front of them, and Cookie continued to glare.

"Huh, you don't look like friends to me. But then again, this is how you looked when you all pretended to be my friend."

That's when the room erupted.

"How could you write that article?"

"Who said you could use my words?"

"I never said that!"

"You threw us all under the bus!"

"I did not have a second facelift!"

"Ha!"

"You called us Lunch Ladies on Good Morning America!"

"How dare you talk about us on TV, you traitor."

"I did not!"

"You did too!"

"I did not!"

"Shut up!" Sandra yelled, and for some reason everyone stopped. Audrey held back the tears. She remembered the essay she had written on a whim and sent to the New York Times. The editors loved it; it went viral on Twitter. She was just starting her TV show and she made a good interview. The View called; so did Good Morning America, Ellen and even Howard Stern. SNL did a skit called Lunch Ladies about actual cafeteria lunch ladies who dressed in couture and hairnets and met in the lunchroom after the kids were back in class to dish on each other. Tina Fey played Audrey. Jimmy Fallon played Cookie.

Ladies Who Lynch

By Audrey Walsh

In high school, I always wanted to be popular. I had some great friends, but we hung on the fringe, wearing almost the right clothes and invited to a few of the many parties. We spent our days watching the well-liked girls move through the halls like movie stars while we hung in the background as extras.

It was ten years ago that I somehow found myself making friends with women who had been popular at their respective schools— the former homecoming queens, cheerleaders and beauties. We were different ages, but it somehow didn't matter— to me— I was accepted and I finally felt like I belonged. We called ourselves the Ladies who Lunch, but I never liked that name much, so I quietly called the group the Lunch Ladies.

For the next decade, I would gather with these women and meet for lunch, and over the years our group grew to include more pretty women, but some, I found, could be very ugly.

When the others were too busy to meet, knives would fly. Gossip and questions would be volleyed back and forth about the state of the MLA's marriages, who might be gay, who was fat and who needed a facelift. It was attack mode for two hours straight. The lunches were often uncomfortable for me, and I felt like a traitor to those who weren't there to defend themselves, but still I showed up.

Last year I sat at a table in an upscale restaurant in Los Angeles waiting for the Lunch Ladies to arrive for a dinner date.

I had moved to New York the previous year, following a job in TV. I said goodbye to friends, family and a fiancée. I missed everyone, but now that I was working on my own show, I could afford to fly back a few times a year to visit. A few months earlier, the Lunch Ladies and I had met up in Manhattan; we shopped and ate and drank our way through the city.

I hadn't seen them since, and for some reason I was apprehensive.

The women arrived within minutes of each other, hugging and air kissing, and then the Queen Lunch Lady herself made a grand entrance.

"Sorry I'm late, but I had to decide what color of upholstery I wanted for my new BMW."

This was her greeting, but I wasn't surprised. We always had to stop our conversations when she arrived to talk about her new house or Botox or travertine tile or waxing or colonoscopy procedure. I let her go on for a few minutes about the car, hurt that she hadn't even asked how I was doing. I then took a deep breath and a big chance.

"Can we talk about something else other than your new car?" I asked.

The women all looked at me as if I had belched loudly.

"I mean, I thought we had some issues to discuss tonight. Your sick parents? Her shaky marriage? My still raw break-up."

I desperately hoped no one noticed that my armpits were sweating as I waited for someone to break the silence.

One of the older women finally spoke.

"I don't think the president is doing what he said he would do," she said not looking at me. "I mean, the jobs aren't coming back and unemployment just keeps getting worse and worse."

"Actually it is getting better," I offered.

"What, you're an authority on unemployment now?" she snapped.

I looked at the other women, who sat staring at me. No one was smiling, and it took me a minute to get my bearings.

"Well actually, I guess I am," I said. "I sat in for the anchor on CNBC one week and did a story on it, remember?"

But they ignored me and started talking about something else as I sat stunned. I watched them toss their over-processed hair and noticed the angry lines etched on their faces and it finally dawned on me. They weren't popular anymore. This group was all that they had left of their former lives. I finally admitted to myself that I was embarrassed to be part of their group.

"Excuse me," I said interrupting. "Did I say something that wasn't true? I mean, have any of you even seen my show?"

Nothing.

"OK," I said taking the plunge. "So you never bothered to watch it. Thanks. Now that we have that on the table, I've been wondering why you've been so unsupportive of how I've finally achieved my dream of having my own show. I mean, why is it that when we flew to New York for the launch you went out to dinner and not to the launch party? I mean, my show is the reason you flew out, isn't it?"

They looked at each other without a spark of guilt.

"We thought it would be best if we didn't," said the Queen. "That way, when no real celebrities showed up, you could come back and embellish the details. We didn't want to be embarrassed for you."

And with that, they went back to talking about the Queen's latest make-up tricks. I, for once, was speechless, and just a little bit dizzy. I looked around at the other tables of people enjoying their food. Laughter filled the large room, but at our table, the bitterness just hung in the air like cheap perfume as I realized I didn't belong. I had never belonged, and we all knew it. I was ashamed at myself for even attempting to be a part of their club. I was embarrassed I had sat in on their attack sessions of other women that I liked and respected and never came to their defense. As they chatted back and forth ignoring me, I slowly reached for my purse. I took a deep breath and one last look before I stood and walked away from the table and out of the restaurant.

I later found out that it took the Lunch Ladies an hour before they noticed that I was gone.

II

Look at us, just like we were at the end. This is what happened after you walked away, Audrey, we started going for each other's throats," Sandra continued.

"Oh please, we were happy she left the group," Cookie said. "She was a pain in the ass. Always the shit-stirrer with her smart-ass remarks."

"I'm pretty sure you started it Cookie," Tracy said quietly.

Cookie, turned on her friend, eyes flashing.

"Sorry, did you say something?"

"I said, you were mad at her for something, which— if you think about it — was ironic, since you had an affair with her fiancée."

Cookie rolled her eyes, but she blushed.

"I'm pretty sure Audrey is over that mistake. I mean, the man came on to me and I almost did the deed with him but I stopped it. It's not like we had a real affair."

"It lasted six months," Audrey mumbled. Cookie ignored her.

"It's not my fault that Audrey couldn't forgive him. It's not my fault he moved out and it's not my fault he got married to someone else so quickly." She looked at the other women, who avoided her eyes. "In all actuality, I think I saved Audrey many years of misery in a loveless marriage." She stared back at Audrey. "He never really loved you, but I'm sure you knew that before we, umm, had our little fling."

Audrey turned her back so that her tears were hidden from Cookie. "It's more than that and you know it," she said quietly. Cookie ignored her.

Tracy took a breath and continued. "You never felt bad about hurting her and yet she kept coming to our lunches. It seemed to me that you continued to kick her when she was down. Anytime she missed a lunch, you made sure to tell the other women things she had said behind their backs, although some of the stuff you made up. Remember? We talked about it when we were at the gym that time I met that cute guy?"

"Oh, what guy was that? Are you still seeing him?" Cookie asked snidely.

Tracy ignored her, excited that she was standing up for herself and even Audrey.

"Remember how you made her cry at happy hour at Tito's?"

"I do," Mattie said. "That sucked."

Cookie turned her head.

"Oh, who cares what you think," Cookie stated. "You stay out of this."

"But I am a part of it," Mattie said. "You trashed Audrey and she finally got the balls to leave. Then you started trashing me and then everyone started trashing everyone else. When Audrey wrote her article everyone turned on each other and that was the end."

"Well not quite," Jerdie said. "When she went on TV and then Laverne and Justine went on too, then that was the end."

"Really? That's how you remember it?" Belinda said. "I remember Jill giving some of you inside information that her winery was going public and leaving the rest of us out. That's when I decided I'd had enough of you *brujas.*"

"Why is she speaking Spanish?" Jill asked, trying to deflect the conversation away from Belinda's memory.

"That's right, you did leave some of us out, like me," Justine said. "I could have used that money. I was hurting and I couldn't always afford to come to those lunches. Why did you leave some of us out? I know that Jerdie and Laverne and Sandra made out like bandits. Hell, that's how Sandra started her makeup line, and Jerdie bought a house in Aspen and Laverne probably bought 20 cases of gin."

"Screw you, Justine."

"You're not my type Laverne."

"Congratulations, we've been in the room for 10 minutes and you've already annoyed me five times," Laverne replied.

"OK, let's stop this bullshit," Cookie said. She walked into the middle of the group. "This is obviously the reason the producers wanted us on the show. They knew we wouldn't come if we knew who would be on this island. I say we grit our teeth and give them the vixens they want us to be. We'll be stars and make a lot of money. We'll be on the cover of *US Magazine* and on other TV shows. I'm in if you are."

"I don't know," Audrey said. "It hurts to remember how close we used to be back then. Now you want us to show the world what shallow and terrible friends we are?"

"Why not?" Cookie said. "You can be a bigger star on TV and act all superior—just like you used to. Something, by the way, I do not miss."

"Hey," Mattie called out from the terrace. "Look at this sunset, it's magnificent."

Belinda turned her head and whistled.

Jill and Tracy walked out together. Tracy managed to smile at Jill, who in fact had not included her in the insider trading, but she didn't care. Well, she did, but there wasn't anything she could do about it now. Jill's assets had been taken away from her as part of the civil suit after her trial, so she was in the same boat herself. She didn't want to say out loud that Jill deserved to lose everything. Instead, she would focus on the positive; the sunset was stunning. In the long run, this place might be good for everyone.

Tracy continued to study Jill as she watched the sun fall slowly from the sky. Although her face stayed frozen, Tracy was sure she saw a tiny smile squeeze through.

The ten vixens stood on the terrace, drinks in hand, as the sun dissolved into the horizon and filled the sky with ribbons of pink and orange, each woman deep into her own thoughts. Audrey was the last one to join the group and she stood back a few paces. Her head throbbed and her stomach growled. This wasn't how she expected this to turn out, but what the hell. She had made her decision and now she was sticking to the plan.

"Is anyone else hungry?" she asked.

III

Dinner—along with pre-made pitchers of cocktails, imported bottled water and Prosecco—was discovered by the hungry reality show contestants. It was laid out in a massive walk-in refrigerator at the far end of the kitchen. The producers had prepared a feast on silver platters that impressed even the most discerning vixen.

The menu, written on thick pink parchment paper, was placed on the massive teak and marble bar. It read:

Vixen Dinner Menu Day One Starters: Selection of Cold Canapés:
Smoked Salmon Spread in Pastry Cups
Prosciutto Wrapped Rockmelon
House Marinated Olives
Lychee Martinis

—

Hawaiian-Style Tuna Tartare (Ahi Poke)
Prosecco

—

Chunky Gazpacho

Asian ⌐. /
Pinot Noir

—

Limoncello Semifreddo with Macerated Berries
Ice cold Limoncello

—

Almond and Rosewater Filled Fresh Dates
Pink Moscato

Next to the menu were ten different colorful hand-painted wine glasses, each depicting beautiful women dressed in form-fitting gowns. The word 'vixen' was outlined in glittery paint on each glass.

"Cute, but a little tacky, don't you think?" Cookie asked. She thought for a moment. "In my bedroom there's a poem or a limerick in a frame on the mantle about 10 little vixens. It's kind of creepy."

Sandra said, "In my room too."

"And mine."

"And mine."

Everyone joined in.

"I think they're meant to be a decoration," said Audrey, trying to move the vixen stemware, which seemed glued to the bar. "I saw some

Riedel glasses in the dining room, we can use those.

"Hell, at least there are plenty of bars in this place," Laverne said a little too loudly. She raised her glass and caught a few smiles. The women were hesitant, but in better spirits than when they had first encountered each other.

After the sun set, the moon had come up quickly; a warm breeze filtered in through the gauze curtains. The women had filled their plates with the a variety of food and sat scattered around a large dining table made of recycled boat wood painted in muted colors surrounded with soft cream-colored chairs with matching velveteen cushions.

Tracy was sipping a martini and cracking jokes as usual, amusing Justine and Belinda.

"So, have you heard about the new Aging Gracefully Barbie dolls?" She asked. "Divorced Barbie sells for $199.99 and comes with Ken's house, Ken's car, and Ken's boat. Recovery Barbie shows how too many parties have finally caught up with the ultimate party girl. Now she does Twelve Steps instead of dance steps. Clean and sober, she's going to meetings religiously. She comes with a little copy of *The Big Book* and a six-pack of Diet Coke. Post-Menopausal Barbie wets her pants when she sneezes, forgets where she puts things, and cries a lot. She's sick and tired of Ken sitting on the couch watching the tube and clicking through the channels. Comes with Depends and Kleenex. As a bonus this year, the book, *Getting in Touch with Your Inner Self* is included. Last but not least, there's Mid-life Crisis Barbie—she thinks it's time to ditch Ken. Barbie needs a change, and Alonzo—her Mexican gardener—is just what the doctor ordered, along with Prozac. They're hopping in her new red Miata and heading for Santa Fe to open a B&B. She includes a disc of, *Breaking Up is Hard to Do*."

The women laughed and sipped their drinks while Jill blushed and Jerdie rolled her eyes and smiled. Mattie and Justine moved to the dark purple sofa and began to talk quietly while Cookie got up to refill her wine and watch the vixens from the dining room entrance.

"It wasn't a Miata, it was a Porsche, wasn't it Jill?' Cookie asked sweetly.

"You don't have to like me, Cookie. I'm not a Facebook status," Jill said, not looking at her former friend.

Jerdie and Sandra both stood up from the table. The large sliding doors were open to the lanai. The sound of the ocean crashed continuously on the rocks below, rising up to the house and carried across the room.

"I love that sound," Mattie said.

"I hate it," Cookie said sharply.

Mattie looked at her in surprise. Cookie's mouth was pinched. "I just can't imagine being here in a storm," she said

"I'll bet they close this place up in the winter," Jill said, glad the conversation had changed. Laverne strolled to the windows and looked down at a steel statue by the pool, wondering if it was supposed to be a woman or a man. Art, shmart, it was ugly. Belinda took a sip of her Moscato and surveyed the room. While it seemed the women were getting along, she knew it wouldn't take much to set someone off and get the whole damn group screaming at each other again. She hoped they could all get along—they could get a lot of money or fame from the show. Besides, the food was delicious. While the company was suspect, they were on a luxurious island and about to become minor

TV stars. Or celebrities, or whatever the press would eventually label them. An easy laugh echoed across the room as the waves continued to thunder down below.

Without warning, a voice, inhuman and penetrating...

"Ladies, vixens! Silence please!"

The women were startled. They looked around and then at each other, at the walls and the ceiling, looking for speakers.

The voice continued- a high, clear female voice.

"You are charged with the following crimes;

Justine O'Keefe, on January 13, 2007, you caused the death of Alexandra Chapin.

Jill Allen, on July 5, 2010, you caused the death of Cherry Williams.

Sandra Baxter, on March 4, 2001 you were responsible for the death of Tina Van Steel.

Matilda Foley, you killed Aaron Schneider on December 11, 1985.

Belinda Rios, on April 1, 2004 you killed your business partner Jonathan Armstrong.

Laverne White, you deliberately killed your husband's lover, Christopher Marston on January 9, 1998.

Tracy Morrow, on September 5, 1995 you caused the death of Ken Gordon.

Jerdie Washington, this year you caused the death of your sister Birdie Rogers.

Audrey Walsh, on August 14, 2012, you were responsible for the death of George Austin.

Cookie Armstrong, on June 5, 1989 you murdered Heather Jackson.

Prisoners of the island, do you have anything to say in your defense?"

IV

The voice stopped.

There was a moment of stunned silence and then all hell broke loose.

"What in the name of God is going on here?" Laverne yelled. "Who was talking? Who is here with us?

Jill was pale and could barely find her voice; "Is this a practical joke?" Her hand holding her drink shook.

Cookie's shoulders sagged and she held onto the counter of the bar, afraid she would pass out. Everyone except Sandra and Audrey were freaking out. Sandra sat in a chair, upright, her head held high, although her cheeks had turned crimson. Audrey observed the room, her eyes active, darting around, puzzled, but going into investigative journalist mode.

"Who the hell is in charge here? Why don't we see anyone else other than us? Where are the fucking cameras?" shouted Jerdie.

"That didn't sound like any of us," Tracy said softly.

Mattie walked around the room and searched the outlets until she found a small iPod speaker. "Here it is," she said loudly. She pushed the button and immediately they heard, *"Ladies, vixens! Silence please!"*

Belinda yelled, "Turn it off! Turn it off, it's horrible!"

Mattie obliged and Justine said, "Pretty tasteless joke."

"You think it's a joke?" Audrey asked.

"Duh, of course it is," Justine replied. "Isn't it?"

V

Jill stood up from her chair, sat down and stood back up.

"This whole damn thing is ridiculous, spreading lies and accusing us of murder," she laughed nervously. "Are we being punked? Is this that kind of show? This producer, Ms. Owens, whoever she is can be sued for libel, I mean..."

Justine interrupted. "That's just it, who the hell is she?"

"I think we need to share information and figure out why we're really here," Audrey said. "Let's all get a fresh drink and compare notes."

"I'll grab us some wine," Tracy said, walking out of the room for a moment and returning with two bottles of Ramey-Hyde Chardonnay. Laverne walked to the bar, and topped off her gin and tonic.

"OK, let's all tell the story of how we were invited and share any information about the producer of the show."

There was a moment of silence and then Sandra spoke. "Fine, I'll start. I received an email from a person named Una Owen explaining that we had met at last year's Beauty Expo and she wanted me to supervise the makeup here on this show, while promoting my line, Hell's Angels. I'm pretty sure I've never met anyone by the name of Una, although have heard of Uma Thurman, but of course she's not setting this up."

Audrey looked at Justine and nodded.

"Me? Oh, well, I got an email pretty much like that from a women named Una Nancy Owen, asking me to show some gals on a reality show how to play golf," she said. "Crap, I'll bet there's not even a damn course on this island. I can't believe a place this classy wouldn't at least have an executive course."

"Stay focused Justine."

"Fine, OK. I never talked to the woman, I only got the email and a plane ticket. Oh, and she mentioned a gal I used to give lessons to, so that made it more legit."

Laverne broke in. "I was told my sorority sisters would be here. She mentioned a few of them so I figured what the hell. Fred thought it would be good for me to get away. I should have known something was up. My sorority sisters hated me."

Belinda snickered.

"Excuse me?" Laverne said. "You have something to add?"

"Me? Sure. I got invited by this chick who signed her email, U.N. Owen, *gringa* name I guess, to be on this reality show, 'Hot Vixens of the Restaurant World,' about female chefs and restaurant owners. I wrote back and told her I'd swim all the way to Australia to be on a reality show, but she sent a ticket and until I saw all of you I was enjoying the hell out of this place."

"Get over yourself," Sandra muttered.

"Oh hell, we've been duped," Cookie said, flinging back her hair again, and setting her pointy chin at Audrey. "This woman, or man or whoever, used different names, but they all sound the same. Or at least the initials. We saw a chance to be on TV and we all fell for the scam. Whatever kind of scam it turns out to be."

"I think you're right Cookie," Audrey said.

"Of course I'm right, you're not the only smart person here ya know."

Audrey ignored the jab and walked over to a desk, found the pen and paper she was looking for and sat at the table. The other women walked closer to her.

"Look here," she said, writing out the different names that the producers had used. "Una Nancy Owen - Una N.Owen- U.N.Owen- each time, or if you stretch it, UNKNOWN!

Jerdie yelled: "Holy Shit."

"Goddammit!" said Justine.

"Dios mío!"

"Yep," said Audrey, "It seems we have been invited to this island and set up by a crazy-ass psycho."

CHAPTER FIVE

I

The women were momentarily quieted as they digested the information. Some looked at each other; others looked out into the night. Audrey spoke again.

"OK, so I need to be upfront about something." All eyes were on her again. "While I was on the plane I received an email from Ms. Owen, telling me there would be a story for me here, something that I would want to investigate and possibly go on the air with it. She actually told me about all of these crimes and explained that the women who committed them would be on this island, but she didn't reveal your names. I thought they would be journalists. I should have guessed."

Immediately the women began yelling.

"Selling us out again, Audrey?"

"What the hell is wrong with you, are you nuts?"

"Backstabbing bitch!"

"It's all a bunch of lies," Cookie shouted over the women.

"We never did any of those things," Jerdie said hoarsely.

Audrey held up her hand.

"Calm the hell down," she said. "Give me a minute to talk and then you can all attack me, just like old times," she said. "If you remember, our unknown friend also said I caused the death of a man named George Austin."

"Did you?" Justine asked.

"Well…some people think I did," she said.

"Holy shit, you killed someone? I knew you had it in you," Laverne slurred. "You can't trust a Democrat."

"Shut up Laverne and let me finish."

"Screw you," Laverne whispered.

"Anyway, three years ago I did a story about a Florida woman who was brutally stabbed in her bedroom one morning. George was the husband of the victim and at work. He had an alibi. The cops grabbed a kid with a drug problem who they found in the area. He had done yard work at the victim's house and knew where the key was, so they took him in, arrested him and the jury found him guilty. I interviewed him on death row. I also interviewed the husband and then spoke to his secretary, who came clean on camera. She said that she lied for him because they were sleeping together. Seems Georgie ran home and killed his wife and then came back and boffed his girlfriend."

"Oh, I remember that one," Tracy said. "I watch all your shows."

"Excuse me?' Cookie said, shooting Tracy an evil look.

"Anyway," "Audrey continued. "George blew his brains out moments after I interviewed him and told him what his former girlfriend had said. Some of the papers said I killed him, but that was just to sell papers. What really happened is that the kid on death row got a new trial and they found him innocent. So did I have a hand in Mr. Austin's death? Maybe. But I also saved a life."

"Oh spare us," Cookie said. "You always come out on top no matter what's thrown your way. My husband said you should have been fired for telling him and blamed you for his death. My husband also said the other guy probably did it and you had no right to interfere. My husband, as you well know, is a very good lawyer."

"Your husband is an ass," Audrey said calmly.

"What the hell did you say?"

"You heard me. He used to be a sanctimonious ambulance chaser and now he makes millions off gullible young athletes as their agent."

"Shut up you two," Justine said. "We need to process this. Audrey, did you know this guy George was suicidal, or that he could harm himself? Did you call the cops before you accused him?"

Audrey thought it over for a moment. "No, I had no idea he would kill himself. I'm a reporter, not a jury. His conscience obviously got the better of him and he knew he would go to prison. I don't feel any guilt for his death."

Jill, who stood away from the group muttered, "You're lying about something, I know you're lying."

II

Justine spoke softly. "I want to tell you about Alexandra Chapin. We were both in a tournament at the Dinah Shore in Palm Desert. She was only 19 and she was a pain in the ass. We were paired up and both doing great, leading the pack. Alex shot a 7-under 65 and had a one-stroke lead. She kept talking smack to me. She was really getting on my nerves. Anyway, we were neck-in-neck all the way to 17. There was a lot riding on the win. Big money, TV time, all that. I was nervous. I was starting to sweat. You remember that I tend to have over-active glands? Do you remember? Anyway, Alex was behind me about 10 yards and I was on the T-box and on my backswing, my driver flew out of my hands and went whipping toward Alex. Hit her right in the forehead and she dropped like a bag of rocks. She was dead before her caddy could get to her. It was terrible. I felt horrible, but everyone saw that it was an accident. Unfortunately, they also called the tournament and no one won that year, but I was the winner. They built a new bar on the 19th hole and named it the Chapin Lounge. Even though everyone knew it was an accident, I was officially banned from tournament play. That's when I started teaching around the state. When our little group here disbanded, I went to LA to run my dad's course. I still feel bad about Alex, but it kind of ruined my life, too."

Most of the women stood staring at her.

"Jesus," said Belinda. "Pity party much?"

"What?"

"Seriously? It's all about how it ruined your life, not that it ended that poor kid's life. I mean, how sweaty were your hands?"

"Very sweaty," "Justine said through gritted teeth. "It's a condition called palmar hyperhidrosis. I get Botox shots to help with the perspiration."

The women snickered.

"What about you Belinda. I read about what you did in the papers. Must be nice to have a good lawyer," Justine said.

"I didn't have anything to do with Jonathon's death. He committed suicide because he sold out to me for practically nothing. He wanted to go off and be a big-time personal chef for that *put a* teen singer Kiki. He was doing her too, when we were partners and living together. "Fine," I said, "go, but sell me the restaurant." And he did—for cheap. Because of pussy. Men are so stupid. Then, when I opened my third place, he came crawling back. "Oh baby, we're a team. Oh baby, I can't cook without you. Oh baby, take me back." I said no. He hired a lawyer and was suing me. Then, one night the idiot kills himself. Eats poison. The cops look at me, sure, but I wasn't even in the same city that night. My lawyer talks to the DA and case closed."

"But didn't he eat baked flan, your specialty?" Jill asked. "I remember you used to make it for our birthdays sometimes."

"Yes Jill, he ate flan," Belinda said, rolling her eyes. "But I didn't make it, he did. And he added rat poison. Ugh, what a terrible waste of flan."

"Whoa," Jill said, stepping away from Belinda. "So fine, my turn to vent. As you all very well know, since this unpleasant business of my divorce and Cherry's death was so vulgar and public I've been through hell and back the past few years. Oh, and by the way, thanks for being there for me at the trial." She looked around at the women who wouldn't meet her eyes. "Oh that's right, you weren't at the trial were you? Except for Audrey who wanted to put it on TV. Fuck you Audrey."

Audrey looked down at her shoes. She held her tongue, not wanting to bring up that Jill's husband had fired her from the magazine that he owned after promising her a dream job as the editor. She quit the *Times* and put away her flak jacket and within months she was unemployed. Henry fired her, sold the magazine and bought the winery. Two weeks later, she found out about her fiancée's affair with Cookie. If anyone had a right to lose their mind, it was her, which she had declared more than a few times over the years.

Jill took a deep breath and continued. "Typical story; the wife helps her husband become successful with a news magazine, working two jobs until it starts making money. Then he throws it all away so he can go into the wine business at age 60. Delayed mid-life crisis I guess, selling the magazine that we started together, and our home, to buy a winery. For three years we struggled and then boom, everyone wanted our wines. It was insane. We hired a huge staff and opened two tasting rooms in Paso Robles. Cherry worked at the office down in Santa Ynez. I stayed in LA to take care of the kids and I commuted up there on weekends, but Henry was up there all the time. Working his ass off. And, as we all found out later, screwing his ass off with Cherry."

"You don't have to continue Jill," Tracy said. "We know what happened."

"Oh do you Tracy? Everyone left me and watched me fall. The thing that hurt the most was that you were the ones who said you'd always be there for me."

"You kind of went crazy, Jill," Laverne said. "We didn't know what to do. You claimed you were mentally exhausted and had blackouts. And, you know, running Cherry over with the grape harvester sounds kind of nuts, and the judge did find you temporarily insane, so nice job there."

"Go have another drink Laverne." Jill said coldly. "As I was saying, you don't understand, after 40 years of marriage he says he was leaving me for an ex-stripper. Named Cherry, and it was her real name!" Jill started to cry. Tracy put her arm around her and she sobbed uncontrollably onto her silk dress.

"Jill's done," Tracy whispered loudly. "Who's next?"

"I'll go," Laverne said in a slow and puzzled voice. "Christopher Marston was a young guy I accidently ran over in Vegas," she said. "It was an accident. He stepped right out in front of me in the parking lot of Mandalay Bay. I didn't see him. It was dark. He was dressed in black."

"You were drunk." Cookie said. "As usual."

Laverne looked at her in defiance. "No one proved I was drunk," she said. "It was an honest mistake. My license was suspended, which I thought was harsh, but I'm a model citizen and I obey the laws of the land. What I don't understand is that the voice said Christopher was Fred's lover. Which is hilarious if you think about it. My Fred? A queer? Maybe the name Christopher confused the crazy voice. Besides, Fred has never cheated on me and it's unthinkable that he would cheat with a man."

Belinda and Jill started to giggle. Then Mattie and then the whole group began laughing at Laverne.

"Oh Laverne, you poor stupid woman," Cookie said. "Fred buys Brawny paper towels for the packaging. He's so gay, Richard Simmons tells him to 'tone it down.'"

The women laughed, although Laverne's shocked face quickly quieted them. Except for Tracy.

"Three friends—two straight guys and a gay guy—and their significant others were on a cruise. A tidal wave came up and swamped the ship; they all drowned, and next thing you know, they're standing before St. Peter," she began.

"First came one of the straight guys and his wife. St. Peter shook his head sadly. "I can't let you in. You loved money too much. You loved it so much, you even married a woman named Penny."

Then came the second straight guy. "Sorry, can't let you in, either. You loved food too much. You loved to eat so much, you even married a woman named Candy!"

The gay guy turned to his boyfriend and whispered nervously, "It doesn't look good, Dick."

The women, even Laverne, laughed loudly. Then she stopped. "Well, anyway, it wasn't my fault."

III

Jerdie spoke next; "So, here's the thing. That stupid voice accused me of killing my sister Birdie. Well, news flash, she's not dead!"

"She might as well be," Mattie said.

"I'm not my sister's keeper," Jerdie said, raising her head high. "Just because we're twins doesn't mean I am responsible for her addictions or her choices."

"How do you know she's not dead?" Audrey asked. "When was the last time you saw her?"

Jerdie thought. "Three years ago. Before I moved to Sydney. It was in Chicago a few days before Thanksgiving. She was pretty bad off. I offered her a ride to our nana's house but she just wanted money so I gave her some. Then I went out to dinner with my ex-husband."

"You don't feel responsible because you stole her fiancé? Because you tricked him into thinking she was you and then surprising him after a few dates? You tricked both of them and Birdie took it hard, especially when you and Byron married."

"Oh please, Birdie is a grown woman and she makes her own

choices. She made a bad choice to use drugs and that's that."

What Jerdie didn't mention is that her sister had repeatedly called to ask to come and get her and to take her home to detox, but with Byron there she wouldn't do it. Instead, she dropped her off at the only rehab that would immediately take her in. She later learned that Birdie had been abused at the shady rehab and she ran away one night. Still, not her problem, she thought.

"Wow, you sure have an attitude," Belinda said.

"What, because I'm black I have an attitude?"

"Nice try," Belinda said laughing. "You have an attitude because you're an asshole. And please, you act whiter than I do."

"Say what you want about me, call me what you want to call me, think what you want to think. I don't need you as friends anymore, I am my own friend," Jerdie said.

"So...you don't have any friends?" Belinda said, laughing again and turning away. "Anyway, the voice seems to know everything about us, so maybe your sister died."

Jerdie thought about it for a minute and held back the tears. "Not my problem," she said quietly.

Cookie laughed bitterly. "What a motley crew of law abiding citizens we are," she said. "So fine, you all know my history. The pageant. Heather drowning. The jury deciding it was an accident. Case closed."

"But tell us Cookie," Audrey said. "You always maintain your innocence, but you were the only one who knew which lock was the real lock. How could you have confused the two?"

Cookie glared at her former best friend. "I just forgot." She replied. "I'm a bit of a flibbertigibbet—as you've often said to my face—which I happen to know is a smarty pants way of saying I'm an airhead."

"You didn't answer my question."

"Oh, fine Barbara Walters. I don't know how I got them mixed up. Heather was such a competitive bitch and she was making me so mad the night before, talking about how she knew one of the judges and her mom was a former Miss Kansas and her grandmother was an actress, and blah, blah, blah. I was trying to practice my own talent," she glared at Audrey, "And yes, I had a talent. I performed a Hula dance on roller skates. It was very edgy. I didn't have a lot of room to practice in the hotel, and my tape cassette with my music broke, and it was very stressful for me. The whole thing was nerve-racking. It could have happened to anyone."

"But it happened to you," Audrey said calmly.

"Shut up and leave me alone!" Cookie screamed. "You're such a loser. We didn't even like you very much, but we let you hang out with us. I can't remember why…maybe we felt sorry for you. But whatever it was, we didn't like you and it took you forever to figure it out."

"Then I made the right choice," Audrey replied. "I'd rather be a friendless loser than hang out with women who secretly hate me."

"Stop your bickering," Justine said. "Damn, you always compete to see who can be the most obnoxious. You both win. Let's go back to the confessions, they're a lot more interesting."

"So who's up next? Mattie?"

"I heard the name but I can't place it," Mattie replied. "It's a mystery to me. It was a long time ago. Might be the name of one of my classmates at Wazzu. I'm not sure though. Hard to remember."

"But the voice blamed you," Justine said.

Mattie thought; "*Of course I remember Aaron. The love of my life. Until he broke up with me and announced he had started seeing someone else. Stupid me, I thought we were going camping so he could ask me to marry him. We were at the end of the lake in September and we were the only people in the campground. Not even a ranger was around. We were silly and pretended we lived off the grid and we were the only two people left on earth. We had a terrible fight and he told me he loved someone else and he decided to leave, but before we could pack our bags, Aaron got sick. Oh, it came on so fast —the pain was intense. Our tent was still up, so he crawled into the sleeping bag on the blow-up mattress and I tried to keep his fever down. I suspected that it was appendicitis, but I wasn't 100 percent sure. When the sun went down, he had chills and a fever. I told him it was food poisoning because I didn't want him to panic. My cell didn't work and it was 25 miles to town. I couldn't leave him alone. He was in so much pain; he was so helpless. He was sick all night, throwing up, shaking uncontrollably. He kept calling for someone named 'Sara.' I have no idea who that was, but it certainly wasn't me. He continued to suffer and I promised that I would somehow get help in the morning. By the time the sun came up, he had stopped breathing. The coroner said he died from peritonitis, caused by acute appendicitis with a perforation. I couldn't have done anything for him. At the funeral, a beautiful woman who signed the guestbook as Sara came and sobbed quietly in the back. I ignored her. My life went on and I mourned the love of my life.*"

"Well, the voice was wrong. I had nothing to do with the death of Aaron Schneider."

IV

"**M**y turn," Tracy said with a fake laugh. "Hey, did you hear the one about the lady comic who couldn't get hired in Vegas until someone quit or died? Yeah, you see, the guy comic who had been playing to sell-out crowds at the Rio had a real gambling problem and was cheating at cards. No one caught him until the female comic heard him talking about it. He cheated the casino out of $850,000. Now, the female comic was a real straight shooter and felt she had to tell the casino bosses that they were being taken for fools by one of their employees. The bosses then took the male comic for a ride in the desert and suddenly there was a spot of for the female comic. The punch line to that story is that the lady comic is me."

The room was silent.

"Damn, that's not funny," Jerdie said. "I thought you were all sweet and innocent. I knew Cookie was a heartless bitch, but I had no idea."

Tracy looked over at Cookie, who turned her back and walked toward the bar.

The women were quiet. One by one, they looked over at Sandra.

She ignored them for a minute or two, then her mouth hardened and her eyebrows rose on her smooth, shiny forehead.

"Are you waiting for my confession? I have nothing to admit," she said.

"Seriously, that's your story and you're sticking to it?" Audrey asked.

"I have nothing to admit and nothing to say about the accusation," Sandra said coldly, crossing her arms over her chest.

The women looked at each other, some bursting with questions, but Sandra sat unyielding and they were intimidated by the former nun.

"OK...so I guess that's that. We all have our explanations and hopefully the confessions are not going to be aired on the show," Audrey said.

"I don't know about you, but I'm leaving the island tonight," Justine said, as she stood and walked to a window that faced out toward the far-away lights of Sydney.

"How are you going to do that?" Belinda asked. "Swim? There are no planes or boats here. I watched the helicopter leave while I was dressing for this lovely reunion."

"We don't have cell phones, but we can email the cops or authorities or someone to get us out of here," Jill said causally.

"Won't work," Jerdie said. "I tried earlier to email my secretary. There's no Internet. No phone and no TV. Other than smoke signals, it looks like we're stuck here until the voice decides to stop filming, or start filming, or do whatever it is that she's going to do with us."

"I don't know, but I think it's kind of thrilling," Laverne said. "It's like a detective story. Very mysterious. You should be writing this shit down, Audrey."

"At this time in my life I have no desire for thrills," Jill said acidly.

"Hell, you're getting too serious for your own good," Laverne said, laughing with a hiccup. "You're not being very vixen-like. You're boring and old. Let's kick it up a notch and figure out what the hell is going on and then we can kick some ass. Hell, here's to a real vixen mystery!"

Laverne picked up her full glass of G& T and downed it. Too fast, because she choked. Her face contorted, turned purple and her eyes popped. She gasped for breath, then slid down her chair. The glass fell, shattering loudly across the floor.

CHAPTER SIX

————

Laverne — Dead

I

It was so unexpected that the women stood still in shock and looked stupidly down at Laverne. Finally, Mattie made her way to the vixen and knelt down beside her, taking her hand in hers, and felt for a pulse. When she looked up at the bewildered group, she wasn't sure how to deliver her news, so she just blurted it out.

"Holy shit, Laverne is dead!"

It took a moment for it to sink in—and then it did.

"Oh my God, what happened?"

"Did she have a heart attack?"

"You can't just keel over like that and be dead."

"Well, she was old."

"She was 62! That's not old!"

Mattie searched Laverne's face. She sniffed at the blue twisted lips, picked up a shard of the glass, touched it with her finger and carefully placed her finger to her tongue. Her expression changed.

"You mean she choked on her gin and tonic?" Cookie asked.

"I don't think she choked."

"Well what then?"

"The sting of death is sin, and the power of sin is the law," Sandra said bowing her head and playing with cross around her neck.

"Shut up, Sandy," Audrey said. "Not the time."

"Nope, she didn't die of natural causes. I am sure about that," Mattie said, gently closing Lavern's eyes with her fingertips.

"Was there something in her drink?" Justine asked quietly, peering over the dead body.

"It sure looks like it. I don't know what it was, but it points to a form of cyanide. It acts instantaneously."

"It was in her glass?" Audrey asked moving a piece of glass with her toe.

"It looks like that to me," Mattie said.

Audrey walked to the bar and removed the cap to the gin and smelled it. Then she carefully tasted it. Then she did the same to the tonic.

"They're both OK."

"You mean she poisoned herself?" Jill asked.

Audrey hesitated. "I guess she did. I don't know what else to think."

"You mean she killed herself?" Belinda said. "Damn, I didn't mean to make fun of her and Fred."

"Of course you did," Cookie said, stomping back into the room and plopping down in a chair. "We all did. It's what we do. Sheesh, she didn't have to kill herself over us."

"Get over yourself Cookie," Jerdie said, staring hard at the beauty queen. "I'm sure she didn't care about what we said. Or at least not so much as to kill herself over us."

"Ha! Trust me, we were all she had in regards to friends," Cookie said, sneering right back at Jerdie. "God, she was always inviting herself over to dinner to our house and nagging us to come on cruises with her and Fred. Ugh. I couldn't stand her. She made herself into our lunch secretary. As if we didn't know how to send our own damn emails out. She was so irritating."

"Wow." Tracy whispered, shivering slightly.

"Could it be something other than suicide?" Audrey asked, walking closer to the body.

Mattie shook her head. Audrey looked around at the other women. Some shrugged their shoulders and others just stared back at her in bewilderment. They had all seen Laverne pour her gin and tonics from the same bottle throughout the evening. No one else drank the gin or tonic; they were usually wine drinkers after dark, except for the deceased. She must have put the poison in her drink herself. But why would she commit suicide?

"You know, it doesn't make sense that Laverne would kill herself," Justine said, pretending to swing a golf club. "She wasn't the type. She'd just drink more."

Mattie thought about it for a moment and walked away from Laverne's body.

"I don't know what to think," she said staring at the floor.

II

Mattie, Justine and Tracy lifted Laverne from the chair as gently as they could and walked slowly toward the staircase carrying her body. The remaining women sat at the dining table and picked at their food.

"I guess her head should go first, so I'll lead," said Justine, who held Lavern under her armpits. "Go slow, there are a lot of stairs and I'm ass-backwards."

"Gotcha," said Tracy, who held onto a leg while Mattie held onto the other. "Don't bump her head on the stairs."

Mattie giggled. "It's not like she can feel it."

Justine laughed, "It's not like she could feel it when she was alive, since she was drunk most of the time."

"Stop, I'm going to drop her," Tracy said, pausing near the top to catch her breath and to stop laughing.

"Oh my God, this is so sad and funny at the same time," she said.

"OK, everyone take a deep breath and get real, we have a dead vixen on our hands. I mean in our hands. Oh shit," said Justine, breaking out in laughter. "Just don't drop her, she's had a bad day."

All three women laughed as they struggled to the top of the stairs. Luckily, Laverne's room was the first one on the right. Tracy turned the doorknob and the women tottered into the room and glanced around, still holding the dead body.

"Gross," Justine said as she took in the décor. Although the room was tastefully decorated in vintage bamboo, including a king-size four-poster bed and matching Chinese Chippendale chairs, Laverne had added her own touches to the boudoir.

Multiple photos of Fred in various states of dress, including a tuxedo, a bathing suit and only a towel, sat on her nightstand, the desk and on her dresser. A red light bulb had replaced the halogen bulb in her bedside lamp, and a glittery sheer robe and gold slippers with fur pom-poms were on top of the green suede ottoman. The elegant bedspread that had originally been on the bed was in a corner of the room on the floor, and in its place, a fleece blanket decorated in animal print covered the mattress while black silk encased the pillows.

"Oh my," Mattie said. "This is different." The women stared. Tracy cleared her throat.

"Should we put her under the covers?" She asked.

"I doubt she'll get cold," Justine replied.

"No, I mean, she's going to get all gross-looking and smelly. Why don't we cover her up like a mummy?"

"And crank up the AC," Justine added.

Mattie pulled back the blankets and they placed Lavern gently on her black silk sheets and tucked her in like a child.

"At least she can't slide off those sheets now," Tracy said. The women chuckled, walked out of the room and shut the door on Laverne.

III

When they returned to the Great Room, they found the other women still in their seats and silent. Their wine glasses sat untouched and a few of the vixens were shivering.

"This is scarier than when Maggie died," Belinda said. "I mean, everyone knows that she was collecting rocks and fell off a cliff and it was a terrible way to die, but at least we weren't there to see it happen."

"Rock hounding," Audrey said quietly.

"What?"

"She was rock hounding, which means collecting rocks."

Belinda rolled her eyes. "Jesus, whatever, she still died. She was the first in our group to die and it was sad, and we never saw her again. This time we watched someone we know choke to death and now she's upstairs rotting away."

"Do you want to have a little funeral for her?" Mattie asked.

"You mean like the one that Cookie held for Maggie at her house in Santa Barbara? I think not. That's something I would like to forget."

Cookie folded her arms over her chest and ignored the comments. The other women had pressed her to plan Maggie's celebration of life at her home, *Casa de Aquarius.* Even though they weren't the best of friends when she died, they convinced her to plan it, mainly because she had the best house. Cookie couldn't remember what it was that made Maggie mad at her, but she really didn't care. Some people were so sensitive. The fact that Maggie dressed rather inappropriately during her lifetime made Cookie want to honor her by dressing in the same type of clothing as her departed friend, so she chose a Marc Jacob short skirt that was white and very full with a swirl black design, which was decorated with black sequins. She paired it with a tight black Betsy Johnson halter top, which was accented with a huge sparkly broach right between her breasts. She wore strappy party sandals with sparkly butterflies on the toes. When the guests arrived in their more conservative outfits, she realized she might have made a tiny faux paus, but she wasn't going to give anyone the satisfaction of changing her outfit. What might have been a mistake was allowing her petite Shih Tzu, Monique, to attend the event. How did she know that the normally well-behaved and house-trained dog would decide that it would be an appropriate time to have a bowel movement while Maggie's daughter was giving her eulogy? Other than that, the celebration of life was perfect as far as she was concerned.

"Expecting people of a certain income bracket to bring food to a funeral is just as tacky as expecting guests to bring food to a wedding reception," Jill said. "And calling the newspaper to cover it for the society page was rather rude if you ask me."

"No one asked you," Cookie said and turned her head.

Audrey started to laugh. "Oh my God, how about when Kurt's

cell phone went off while Maggie's mom was crying and trying to read her speech?

Audrey and Tracy started to sing, "*Ah, ha, ha, ha, stayin' alive, stayin' alive.*"

Everyone laughed except for Cookie, who cringed. "Kurt likes the Bee Gee's, what can I say?"

"Worst. Funeral. Ever." Sandra said yawning wide. "No one even prayed."

"I guess we should go to bed," Belinda said taking a hint. "It's after one."

"Yeah, I think we should get some sleep and figure out how to deal with this in the morning," Audrey added.

"I think I'll clean the kitchen," Jill said.

"Oh stop with your OCD," Belinda said. "The dishes will be there in the morning."

"Fine, if it bothers you so much I'll do them in the morning," Jill said, throwing up her hands. "Such bossy women. This is why I have male friends."

"Hey, do any of you have a sleeping pill or a Xanax?" Justine asked. "All this bickering and dying has given me anxiety. Not to mention touching a dead body gave me the creeps. I doubt I'll be able to sleep."

"Ha, there's probably more Xanax in this house than wine," Jerdie said. "I'll give you an Ambien, it's better than Xanax for sleeping. Just don't sleepwalk and drive the golf cart into the ocean."

The women stood and filed upstairs slowly, their heads filled with grave thoughts as they solemnly passed Laverne's door. The house, beautiful and new earlier in the day, now seemed to be scary, full of creaks, drafts and rattles: a house straight from a Wes Craven movie, with the sound of the waves hammering the shore non-stop in the distance.

"This place gives me the creeps," Mattie muttered as she walked into her room.

One by one the others did the same, all locking their doors behind them.

IV

Audrey turned all the lights on in her room and shut the French doors to the balcony. She put a David Bowie CD in the Bose stereo by her bed, and took off her dress and hung it up. She walked into the large bathroom, wiped off her makeup with apple cider vinegar and splashed cold water on her face. She tried to focus on the beautiful bathroom done in an all-white palette with pristine surfaces and fixtures. If it weren't for a dead woman down the hall, she would take a bath and read a book by the light of the statement-making chandelier. Instead, Audrey finished her nightly routine by smoothing coconut oil and Le Mer eye cream on her face, gazed at herself in the mirror and went back into the bedroom. She changed into a Victoria's Secret Sleep shirt and climbed into the king size bed. Audrey then thought about George Austin. She remembered how confident he seemed when she first interviewed him. Tall and tan, with a swagger. He had a full head of blond hair, a straight nose with a few freckles and big sleepy blue eyes. He dressed in a Hugo Boss suit, white collared shirt and cowboy boots. Audrey knew for a fact that he didn't own any cows or horses. He had a habit of looking her right in the eye when he spoke and was straightforward when he answered questions. The cops grilled him for 11 hours, but he never even broke a sweat. He was polite and answered everything in an even-toned voice. He even passed a lie detector test.

George had actually asked to be on TV, and was very excited about appearing on Audrey's show. No one had spoken to him except the cops and a few local TV people, which disappointed him. *Inside Detective* was the big time, it was national, and that matched his ego. What he didn't know was that Audrey had spoken to his ex-secretary/ex-girlfriend Veronica, and she'd retracted his alibi. Audrey's producer warned her that it was 'gotcha' TV and smacked of sensationalism, but hell, it was sweeps week. How was she to know the lying wife-murderer had a permit to carry a gun? Hell, he could have killed her first, but instead, after she sprung the news on him, he gave her a sad little smile, walked off camera, took out his pistol, looked at Audrey and said, "I'm sorry," and shot himself in the head.

Audrey wound her Burberry watch, placed it on the Bose and remembered exactly how she felt when she tracked down Vivian. She took her out for coffee and then dinner. They talked like girlfriends and she had tissues for Veronica when she cried. Actually, she thought Veronica was a first-rate twat for lying and causing young Kyle Benton to go to prison, but damn, she loved investigative journalism.

When George blew his brains out it no doubt shook her up, but in all honesty, she didn't feel bad. He had it coming after killing his wife and letting Kyle take the fall. Luckily for everyone, she had set the record straight.

Audrey got into bed and pulled the sheet over her. Egyptian cotton if she wasn't mistaken. The night had been wild, stressful and downright scary, but she might actually be able to fall asleep. Within minutes she was softly snoring.

V

Tracy tossed and turned in her big, beautiful bed. It was soft, yet firm enough for her back, and the sheets and cotton blankets were top-rate. The A/C was on because she had all the windows closed. She had two lights on in the room as well, so that might have contributed to her restless sleep, but it was really Kenny Gordon who was on her mind. She liked Kenny; they got along great. He had been playing the King's Lounge for three years and didn't look like he was leaving anytime soon. He was funny, not too off-color; the people who wanted to see a show but not spend the big bucks really appreciated him. She remembered her favorite joke he told:

Three buddies decided to take their wives on vacation for a week in Las Vegas. The week flew by and they all had a great time. After they returned home and the men went back to work, they sat around at break and discussed their vacation. The first guy says "I don't think I'll ever do that again! Ever since we got back, my old lady flings her arms and hollers, "7 come 11" all night and I haven't had a wink of sleep!" The second guy says "I know what you mean...my old lady played black jack the whole time we were there and she slaps the bed all night and hollers "hit me light or hit me hard", and I haven't had a wink of sleep either!" The third guy says "You guys think you have it bad! My old lady played the slots the whole time we were there and I wake up each morning with a sore dick and an ass full of quarters."

Oh man, the senior citizens really liked that one. In fact, she used it in her act now.

Previously, she only had one gig a week playing in the Volcano Room at the Casino Royale. It was a tiny, tacky room with a view of the volcano at the Mirage Hotel. If you looked out the window and across the street, you could watch the eruption at the classier hotel. It truly was a sad gig. But she partied with Kenny and a bunch of other comics: they shared dinners at the Peppermill or pancakes at Du-Par's after their spots and went to strip clubs on their nights off. But still, Tracy wasn't making it. She had a part-time job at a 24-hour souvenir shop down by Circus Circus, which she detested. She was ready to pack it in and go home. Until late one night, when she and Kenny were in a cab coming home from dancing and drinking at Gold Diggers, and he started talking about how great he was doing. That wasn't the Kenny she knew, but suddenly he was bragging about his gambling wins and explaining just how he was winning.

"I cheat," Kenny said, laughing hysterically as she exchanged a look with the cabbie in the mirror.

"Jesus, Kenny," Tracy said. "I don't want to know."

"Sure you do," he said. "It was so much fun because I was finally able to put my high school acting lessons to use by pretending to be a drunken tourist gambler. I would stumble over to the roulette table and place a couple of chips down as my bet. The top chip would be a $5 chip, or some other small denomination, but underneath would be a higher value chip. I would place the top chip in a way that the bottom chip couldn't be seen. If my bet lost, I would grab my chips—which you are not actually allowed to do, hence the drunken act—and fling them at the dealer. During this move I would swap the higher value chip for another $5 chip." He laughed and raised his eyebrows at her like Groucho Marx and continued.

"If, however, my bet won, I would make a big deal of celebrating. Invariably the dealer would be a little confused, assuming I had just staked two $5 chips. At this point I would point out the fact that the chip underneath was more valuable. Because I had legitimately placed the bet, even if surveillance was checked by casino security they would find nothing wrong. I was effectively cheating on my losing bets rather than my winning ones, and it's winning bets that tend to be scrutinized."

"Damn, Kenny that sounds dangerous."

"Nah, I'm smarter than those Dagos. Ya see, using this method I've been able to win thousands on my winning bets and lose only a few dollars on my losing bets. I've been doing this from Vegas to Mesquite and down to Stateline. It's foolproof. Hey, don't look so worried about me. I've got this. Come on, let me buy you breakfast. Cabbie, turn us around and take us to the Paris."

After eating a huge omelet at Mon Ami Gabi, Tracy hugged Kenny, went home and climbed into her tiny bed in her equally tiny apartment. After tossing and turning, she finally climbed out of bed and wrote an anonymous letter to the Rio HR department. She outlined exactly what Kenny was doing and how much he was making. She mailed it on her way to the souvenir store. Three days later, Kenny was gone and there was an ad for a comic at the Rio. Tracy had them laughing right away at her interview and got the gig. She quit the Volcano Room and the store and rented a bigger apartment. Life went on and the Kenny rumors ran rampant. Everything from a sighting at a casino in Monaco, to a cruise ship gig, to being buried in the desert. She wasn't a gambler, but she would bet on the desert story. She felt bad about what happened, but she figured Kenny would have been caught at some point. No one knew about her part in it, though, not even Cookie, but someone knew. The voice had blabbed about it and now everyone suspected. Damn it. She had no idea what would happen to her, but she was sure it was going to be bad. She would be known as the joke killer.

VI

Jill Allan thought about Laverne and felt terrible that she wasn't grief-stricken over the death of her former friend. How strange that she killed herself. Could she really have been that upset by their remarks over Fred? Did she really not know he took male lovers? Maybe it was something else. Wow, suicide…that was a bit over the top. She wasn't going to let it get to her because she had just realized that she had been looking forward to getting away and staying on the island for a few months or so. She hoped the 'voice' didn't kick them off the island just because Laverne decided to mess everything up and off herself.

Through the cracked window, Jill could hear the waves crashing on the rocks. The sound was comforting, unlike the sounds of Highway 1 outside her apartment near Fountain Valley. She still missed the sound of the ocean that she used to hear at her condo on the beach in Kihei, the home she had to sell to pay for her defense lawyer. The OC place was situated between two busy restaurants. Even the double-paned windows couldn't keep the traffic noise at bay. This island was, in her opinion, heaven. Maybe she wouldn't go back. Maybe she would stay, even after the show; do something for the owners. Be a caretaker or something. God knows she knew how to care for beautiful homes. So that was that. She'd made up her mind: she wasn't going to leave this beautiful island voluntarily.

VII

Cookie had been staring at the ceiling for two hours, afraid to fall asleep. The light on her nightstand was on, as was the one in the bathroom. She was afraid of the dark and had been for decades. Almost every night, unless she was hammered, she had to block out the memory of the fight she and Heather had an hour before the pageant.

Cookie was losing her confidence, and tried to skate in the small room while Heather practiced yoga, contorting on the floor on a big beach towel. Heather wore a cute belted blue striped thong leotard with pink leggings. Her usual auburn puffy hair was in a ponytail on top of her head. She stretched her strong athletic legs in front of her and Cookie ran into her foot and tripped. The two got into it.

"What the hell is wrong with you?" Heather yelled, jumping up from the floor. "You could go outside and practice that stupid roller dance you've cooked up. By the way, the judges are going to laugh their asses off at your so-called-talent."

"Screw you Houdini." Cookie sneered and rubbed her knee. She found her balance and slowly stood up and faced her roommate. "You have the dumbest talent by far."

"Really?" Heather asked. "I'll have you know that the judge, you know the star of the Singing Factory? Well his step-cousin is David Copperfield."

"How do you know?"

Heather smiled sweetly. "He told me in bed Tuesday night."

Cookie knew she was bested; Heather was going to win the crown. Her heart fell, and then she had an idea...

"No," Cookie said out loud. She brought herself out of the past and back onto the island. "I'm not going there. It's the past. It's over. Done with."

She jumped out of bed to look for another Xanax. She found one and swallowed it without water.

Jesus, Laverne, you really are a dumb bitch, she thought. Why would you kill yourself, and in such an ugly way?

As she passed the fireplace she looked up at the poem again.

'Ten little vixens went out to drink wine;

One choked her little self and then there were nine.'

"OK, that's creepy," she said to herself.

Why the hell did Laverne want to die? She thought. I don't want to die. I want to live forever. I'm going to do everything I can to look 40 until I'm 90. I'm pretty sure I'll outlive all my friends, including all the women on this stupid island.

VIII

Mattie was dreaming about Aaron.

They started out as friends, working on the veterinarian's ranch that summer after college near Wenatchee. They were so happy. She was so happy. Then they went camping and he got sick. His appendix burst and he had to have an emergency appendectomy. Easy procedure. No problem for normal people. She could see him lying there. His face so relaxed. Maybe she could kiss him. No, this was business. He was sick. Where was the doctor? He could die. Wait, did he just open his eyes? Was he angry? She hated it when Aaron was angry. So sharp-tongued. So mean. She looked around the room. Did the nurses notice that he was yelling at her? Did the surgeon? How embarrassing. Aaron was always doing that. But she loved him so much. She had to think. She needed a drink. Just a quick one to calm her nerves. Aaron watched her go. He knew she was drinking too much, but screw him. He couldn't do anything lying on that table. She went outside. Took a drink from her flask. Then another. Maybe even one more. She was so hot, she needed to go for a swim in the lake. She walked down to the shore, put her feet in and stared across at the old brick castle. Maybe she and Aaron could buy it and live happily ever…wait, where was Aaron?

She walked back to the tent. A sheet was covering him. Why? What happened?

"Dead," said a nurse.

"Dead," said the surgeon.

"No, it can't be. I thought he would be fine. I tried to call but there wasn't any reception."

Everyone was smiling at her and she didn't know why. She slowly pulled the sheet off Aaron and jumped back. It was Laverne. She was laughing. Her face was purple and she was laughing. She reached out for Mattie and…

Mattie woke up. She sat up, rubbed her temples and shielded her eyes from the sun. She was drenched in sweat and the sheets were in a knot at the bottom of her bed. She climbed out of bed and threw open the French doors. The sun was shining brightly: not a cloud in the sky. The ocean was a wide expanse of glitter and the brightness of it all made her head throb.

"Crap," she muttered. "Better go easy on the wine tonight."

CHAPTER SEVEN

October 11

I

Belinda was the first person to head downstairs to breakfast. There was freshly brewed coffee in a large stainless steel decanter and she found fruit and yogurt in the walk-in fridge. She was dressed in a sky blue Lululemon yoga onesie and ballet slippers. She had been practicing yoga on her deck, trying to relieve the stress of the night before, but she was still a tight mess.

She padded to the dining room and passed the bar. She stopped for a moment and took a closer look at the vixen glasses, which were still lined up. She gazed at the sparkly paintings of the sexy women on the glasses and then stepped back. She counted.

"Huh," she muttered. "There's only eight."

II

Cookie and Tracy came downstairs together, their heads close and their hands over their mouths.

"Secrets?" Belinda said.

"Nothing that concerns you," Cookie said.

"Oh really," Belinda said, placing her coffee cup in front of the wine glasses. "I would think after last night we might form some sort of bond. You know, to make it out of here alive?"

"Jesus, don't be so dramatic," Cookie said, finding a cup and pouring in hot coffee. "Laverne killed herself because she was an alcoholic and depressed about Fred being a queer." She walked to the bar and poured some Bailey's Irish Cream into her cup and took a sip.

"We need to figure out what kind of game this director is playing. We need to figure out how to get off this damn island and how we're going to play it out to the media."

Audrey snorted behind her.

"Are you serious, Cookie? You actually think the media is going to be interested in you? Why? We have one dead woman and that's the story. Who cares about you? Unless, you know, you want to bring up Heather Jackson again. You want to stir that shit-pot?"

"Was I speaking to you?" Cookie asked, smiling at Tracy and looking anywhere but at Audrey. "I'm pretty sure I made it clear we were not on speaking terms nine years ago when you threw me out of your apartment."

"Because you were being a bitch and I had finally had enough?" Audrey said, looking for some tea. "You mean that night?"

"That's your side of the story," Cookie replied. "And for the likes of me, I'll never forget the first time we met—although I keep trying." Cookie laughed. "I've been meaning to get that zinger out and I finally said it to you."

"Oh, ouch," Audrey said. She turned her back and turned on the stove under the kettle.

Jill and Sandra walked into the kitchen, followed by Mattie and Jerdie. Jill walked over to the bar and began making a Bloody Mary. She poured three shots of Grey Goose Vodka into a tall glass of ice, added a splash of mix and a dash of Tabasco. The other women watched her.

"What?" Jill said pleasantly. "I'm on vacation. Anyone else want a Bloody?"

"Sure, why the hell not?" Tracy said. 'Hey, you know that song by Willy Nelson? How does it go? Oh I know."

'Well, it's a Bloody Mary mornin' Baby left me without warning,
Jill joined in;

113

When they were finished, Audrey and Mattie clapped for the pair.

"That was sweet," Mattie said. "So maybe this means we might be able to have some sort of truce?"

"I don't think so," Jill said, turning her back to make another drink. "You know Mattie, I thought you would be the one person I could count on to stand by me, but you pretended nothing was going on. And that made it worse. To me, your betrayal was worse. You stabbed me in the back 100 times. The worst part was all these other wenches were helping you while I was bleeding to death."

"Wow, that's a little much, don't you think?"

"Really?" Jill screeched. "I needed help and all of my friends abandoned me. It was worse than Henry betraying me. So much worse because I realized you women were never my friends. I told you everything about my marriage and you pretended to care. You knew Henry was cruel to me, treating more like a slave than a wife all those years. How he was so jealous, that I couldn't go anywhere for years without him. How he controlled my every move until he finally found another woman he could control. You enjoyed my status when the magazine was hot and then the winery did well and you enjoyed the free trips, the bottles of wine and the great service at restaurants, but when it came down to it you were using me."

"Excuse me, can we talk about something else?" Sandra said, breaking into the conversation.

"Oh I'm sorry, does the truth hurt Sandra?" Jill asked. "You were horrible as well. You spoke to the district attorney and told him lies about me. I couldn't believe it, and then I did. It's funny how you were nice to my face, hilarious how you talked shit about me behind my back, and it was downright comical that you thought I was unaware of it."

Sandra turned her back on Jill, grabbed a plate and filled it with pineapple, mango slices and papaya.

"Oh yum," she said in a fake happy voice. "Just what I need to make this a great morning!"

"OK, let's talk about how we are going to contact someone and get off this island," Jerdie said.

"Sure professor, are you going to build us a radio out of coconuts and bamboo?" Audrey teased.

"What?"

"You know, *Gilligan's Island*? Hello?"

"Oh sorry, that's before my time," Jerdie shot back.

"Fine," Audrey said carefully. "Do you have a plan?"

"Well, I think we should start by searching the house and then the property. There has to be some sort of communication devices. Planes and helicopters fly into this place, so it makes sense that there's something we can use to communicate with the authorities."

"Not a bad idea."

"Gee, thanks boss."

"You can't be civil?" Audrey asked. "Can no one in this house be nice for five minutes?"

"Whatever, Audrey," Jerdie said. "You're always playing the victim but you weren't the greatest of friends. I mean, I'm not saying you were a bad friend, you just weren't a good one to me."

Audrey observed Jerdie. Her features were much sharper than she remembered. She was still a beautiful woman, but she was too thin, and her cheekbones, her nose and her chin looked like they would cut you if you got too close. She had done something to her face, but maybe not. Perhaps it was stress and not eating enough to stay thin. Although she pretended not to care, she had to have some guilt over her sister. The twins had been close growing up. She remembered Jerdie telling them stories about how they had a secret language before they learned to talk. When they were in fifth grade, and she and Birdie were in the same class, and they had a spelling test. They were on opposite sides of the room; when the test was over they had the exact same mistakes and marks where they scribbled out the wrong answer to correct it. They were both sent to the office, but the principal concluded there was no way they could have cheated. Audrey remembered how sweet Jerdie looked when she told the story and how hard she looked now. Life was obviously not as great as Jerdie made it out to be. But then again, truth be told, whose life was?

"You have nothing to say, Audrey?" Jerdie asked. "Were we that easy to replace?"

"I didn't replace you. I finally realized that I would rather have no friends than nine backstabbing Lunch Ladies."

"Ladies who Lunch," corrected Mattie, pointing her finger at Audrey.

"Oh, that reminds me," Belinda said, pointing to the wine glasses. "Check this out."

"We saw them already," Jill said.

"I know, I know, but do you remember how many there were when got here?" Belinda said.

"10," a few of the women said.

"Right? So how many do you see now?"

They crowded around the table.

"Eight, I count eight," Jerdie said. "Who has the other two?"

They looked at each other.

"Oh wait, maybe Justine took them as souvenirs," Tracy said. "She's not awake yet."

The women scanned the room.

"She's always up early. Maybe she's out hitting balls into the ocean," Audrey said.

"Most likely," Cookie said. "Besides, who cares?"

"You know Cookie, Justine has had a rough couple of years and you know it, so you might try and be a little nice to her," Tracy said. "First her dad died of cirrhosis of the liver, and she barely kept his golf course out of foreclosure. Then her mom was diagnosed with Alzheimer's and that took a toll on her. I know you knew about it. She told me she tried to call you a few times for some help."

Cookie rolled her eyes.

"As a matter of fact she did. She called under the pretense of asking Kurt for some legal advice, but she was really hinting around that we might like to be partners with her in the golf course. Kurt actually thought it might make a fun investment—God knows we can use the right-offs—but I said absolutely not. She got herself into financial trouble because of bad business decisions and I'd be damned if I was going to bail her out."

"I sent her $200," Tracy said. "It was the best I could do."

"Sucker," Cookie said, laughing. The other woman looked away.

"Well, we shouldn't wander off in case someone comes to get us," Tracy said, recovering. "Also, we don't really know what the hell is going on here. Are we in danger? Seriously, who is coming to take us off this island and how long will we be here?"

The women stayed silent or shrugged.

"Fine, I'll go knock on Justine's door and see if she's in there. Anyone want to come with me in case the boogieman gets me?"

"Sure, I'll go," Jerdie said.

"Go ahead, I'll be here enjoying another Bloody Mary and looking out into the ocean," said Jill cheerfully. "Damn it's beautiful here. Have you seen how the water sparkles in the sun? Isn't it beautiful here?"

III

"Mattie, come quick," Jerdie yelled, her voice filled with panic.

Mattie and Audrey's eyes met. She turned and ran out of the kitchen with Audrey on her heels. The rest of the group followed them up the stairs.

"What's going on?" Mattie saw Justine lying on the bed, the covers neatly tucked in around her and a bright pink pillow with white trim lace sitting on her face. The pillow had intricate stitching with the saying, "Keep Calm and Vixen On," facing up.

Mattie looked at the other women, who stood with their eyes wide and their mouths open. She tried to breathe. Her heart beat wildly as she tried to suppress a panic attack. She placed her fingertip on the pillow and gently took it off Justine's face. The women gasped. Justine's face was white, but her eyes were open and blood red. Her nose was purple and bruised.

"Um, did she kill herself too?" Belinda asked quietly.

No one said anything while Mattie felt for a pulse.

"She's definitely dead," Mattie said.

The vixens all stepped forward and moved aside for each other so they could take a look. Tracy stayed back. Her fingers nervously played with her pearl necklace.

"This cannot be happening," she said, her voice shrill. "It's like a joke or something. Can two vixens be dead within 12 hours of each other?"

"But, could she do that to herself? Is it possible?" Belinda asked again.

"No, Belinda, she didn't kill herself, someone else did it. Jesus, how stupid are you?" yelled Sandra.

"OK, OK," Jill said, who had come up after the others, but in time to see Justine's horrible face. "Let's not freak out. There's got to be an explanation for these two deaths."

"The place is haunted, it must be," Jerdie said.

Cookie snorted. "Right. A ghost killed her. What kind of ghost carries a pillow around?"

"I don't fucking know, Cookie," Belinda said. "Do you have any idea what's going on?"

Cookie glared at her.

"So now what?" Audrey asked, looking from vixen to vixen.

"I guess we do that same thing as we did for Laverne. Don't touch anything by the way. This is something the police will want to investigate. Put the pillow back on her face."

"What the hell?" Jerdie asked.

"We might not remember everything, and we don't want to have 10 different stories."

"Eight." Jerdie said.

"What?" Mattie's face flushed. "Oh right. Eight."

Mattie gently rested the pillow back onto Justine's face and Tracy turned the air conditioner to high.

"Should we say something, like a little prayer or something?" Belinda asked.

They looked at Sandra. She rolled her eyes.

"Oh, fine," she said, walking slowly to Justine's body.

"Ahem... 'Not everyone who says to me, `Lord, Lord,' shall enter the kingdom of heaven, but he who does the will of my Father who is in heaven. On that day, many will say to me, `Lord, Lord, did we not prophesy in your name, and cast out demons in your name, and do many mighty works in your name?' And then will I declare to them, `I never knew you; depart from me, you evildoers.' Amen."

"Sweet muppity Christ, could you have said a creepier prayer?" Jill asked. "No wonder you're not a nun anymore."

"Fine, you do it," Sandra said.

Jill thought for moment, then a moment longer, and laughed

nervously.

"I don't know any besides 'Now I lay me down to sleep...'"

"She's already asleep forever. No. Stop," Jerdie said firmly, shaking her head.

"Fine, someone else?"

"I can tell a joke," Tracy said.

"Of course you can," Cookie mumbled. Tracy ignored her.

"That's fine, better than those depressing prayers," Audrey whispered.

Tracy walked to the bed. "I hope you like this," she said to the body. "So, three friends die in a car accident and attend an orientation in heaven. An angel asks, "When you are in your casket and your friends and family are mourning you, what would you like to hear them say about you?"

The first guy says, "I would like them to say that I was a great doctor and a loving family man."

The second guy says, "I would like them to say that I was a caring husband and a schoolteacher who made a huge difference to kids."

The last guy says, "I would like them to say—look, he's moving!"

CHAPTER EIGHT

―――――

Laverne — Dead
Justine — Dead

I

Jerdie and Audrey stood on the lanai drinking mimosas and gazing out at the vast ocean. The water was calm, and slow and steady waves lapped down on the pink sandy beach below. On the other side of the house, waves washed over jagged rocks. Audrey spotted a mix of hard coral in the clear water. It resembled honeycomb that waved back and forth like ferns under the sea.

"Look, that coral looks like flowers, like lavender," Jerdie said, spotting the same underwater display. The gardens above the sea were dotted with colorful bougainvillea and towering coconut palms. There were plenty of hammocks from which to gaze up at the ospreys soaring overhead. Somehow, the island felt both dangerous and calm to Audrey.

"Do you think we can get out of here?" Jerdie asked.

"I'm not sure, but someone's going to start missing us soon. We all have families and people."

"But we told them we wouldn't communicate for two weeks. Lord knows what could happen by then."

"Right, two weeks," Audrey said taking a sip of her coffee. "But you were correct when you said there might be some way to communicate with the police or someone. We need to really scour this place and look for some sort of wireless or phone or something. There has to be some sort of emergency system. I mean, it's an island—they must have issues with power during storms."

"So, you don't think anyone's coming to get us?"

"Of course no one is coming, why would they? We've been tricked." Jill said impatiently as she walked up behind them.

Jerdie turned around. "Really? I mean…"

"Ha, of course not. No one is coming for us. That's the whole point of this charade. We're not going to leave this place…none us will escape…it's over, done with, end of story." She paused and walked closer to the edge. "I bought into a 1950s *Leave It to Beaver* marriage with Henry," she said, "then he stole my whole life."

Audrey and Jill both knew about the breakup of the marriage. The whole world knew; it was front-page news. When Jill found out about Cherry, she broke into her ex-husband's home, smeared chocolate pies in his dresser drawers, rammed her car into his front door, attacked him with a knife, and left expletive-laced messages on his answering machine. They both remained silent.

"We had the perfect marriage," Jill said softly. "I supported Henry while he attended UC Berkley. I raised our two sons almost single-handedly, with little help, while Henry started the magazine. Then, when he had finally achieved everything we scrimped and worked for, he sold it all and bought the vineyard. Then he threw me over for Cherry, his receptionist. To make it worse, he had the balls to torment me in and out of court." Jill was visibly trembling, and stepped back from the edge.

"I like knowing that the end is coming. It's very peaceful, don't you think?" she asked the women, a fake smile on her face.

Audrey looked at Jerdie and back at Jill.

"Are you all right, Jill?" she asked.

"Sure, I'm great," she said, turning and almost tripping on a step. "Actually, I'm fan-fucking-tastic." Then she walked back into the house, her hand waving goodbye.

"Well that was disturbing," Audrey, said shaking her head.

"Umm, you think everyone will start losing it before we get rescued?"

"God, I hope not. We have to keep our sanity and actually stick together."

Jerdie laughed. "It might be easier to swim to Sydney than get along, but I'm game."

125

The two women looked at each other. Jerdie shrugged, stepped forward and gave Audrey a hug.

II

"Oh gross, you're making up," Cookie said. She scrunched up her face as she sauntered out onto the patio. She was wearing gaudy, hot pink and yellow workout pants with a tiny pink bra top and bright orange Nike trainers.

"We're trying to make peace so we can work together to get ourselves out of this place," Jerdie said, trying to ignore Cookie's too-tight top and obvious camel toe.

"Well good for you both," Cookie replied. "I am going to the gym and then for a swim. There's a sauna and an awesome hot tub. You two BFF's figure out a way to get me home while I tone up my abs and relax. *Ciao.*"

Audrey watched her go and sighed. She turned back and stared at the cliffs on the other side of the house. Was one of the vixens walking by the rocks?

Jerdie spoke. "So what the hell really happened with you two? You were good friends, kind of sisters in crime for a few years, even after she almost screwed your boyfriend. Which, by the way, is weird on your part. Who stays friends with the woman who broke up their engagement? Besides that, you're *so* different from each other, but I

127

guess that's what makes up a lot of relationships."

"I don't know, we always had a little love/hate thing going, but it eventually grew into hate," said Audrey. "I started to hate her after Sean and I broke up, but she came at me with fake apologies. I always wanted her to like me and I figured that if my future husband was gone, I might as well bond with my friend. I quickly realized it couldn't work. We're opposite in politics, and she turns her nose up at the poor. She mocked my beliefs. And honestly, she's homophobic and racist."

"Really?" Jerdie said with a half a smile. "I never noticed."

"Oh, right,"

"Anyway, we grew apart. I stopped taking her bullshit and she didn't like it. She wanted to be queen lunch lady and I didn't care, I just didn't like her attitude. Over a year, I guess, we kept arguing when we went out. I thought she was shallow and she thought I was a know-it-all. I guess we were both right. Finally, one night we were both pretty drunk when we got back to my place, and she started in. I tried to defuse it, but she kept at it, kept attacking me. Finally I told her to leave. Kicked her out, actually I shoved her out of my apartment. It was ugly. We were both screaming and I was crying. It was over. Finally over."

"Wow, sounds like an old married couple."

"Kind of, I guess. After that, she seemed to have all of you on her side. I would meet up and get the cold shoulder from Laverne..."

"Laverne is, I mean, was a suck-up," said Jerdie. "Fred had a crush on Kurt and was always pushing Laverne to score an invite to *Casa de Aquarius*. By the way, is Cookie the only person we know who named her house?"

"Right, I know, but slowly I felt you all slipping away from me."

"We actually all had our issues with the group," Jerdie said. "And in life. It's wasn't all about you. Laverne had a breast cancer scare, Belinda's dad fell off that cruise ship, Mattie got hit by a taxi and Jill was still nuts over Henry."

Audrey blushed. "I know. I mean, it was hurtful the way you all stood behind her and it gnawed at me. Finally, after one of the lunches—that one in Laguna Beach, when it was 100 degrees outside and Cookie was hammered and pretending to actually have a conversation with me and everyone seemed so condescending?—that was the last straw."

"Maybe it was the heat. Or the bad tuna melts."

"Maybe," Audrey said, "But when I drove away I knew it would be my last gathering."

"But you were wrong," Jerdie said, finishing her coffee. "This is your last."

CHAPTER NINE

———

I

Sandra eyed Jerdie and Audrey talking outside as she bustled around the kitchen. She filled the dishwasher and wiped down the counters. When she was satisfied, she walked out the sliding teak doors and glanced down the stairs at the beach, where Belinda was patiently waiting for her. Sandra had put on a large sunhat that she found in her room and proceeded down the steps. She was dressed in linen walking-shorts the color of a robin's egg and a white silk T-shirt and wore Tom's grey felt sneakers on her feet. She carefully stepped down the teak staircase to the pool area and glanced over at the workout room. She noticed Cookie huffing and puffing on the epileptic machine. Good for her. She passed the massive swimming pool, which sported a green and grey checkerboard pattern on the bottom designed after 'Yin and Yang.' Palm trees, birds of paradise, and other tropical plants surrounded the lavish pool. The giant whirlpool bubbled happily and looked inviting. The tennis court was clean; rackets stood at attention in a line as if waiting for an impulsive game. The breeze was warm. Walking toward the sand, Sandra was disappointed in herself that she hated to go barefoot. Belinda was sitting on the sand and held Tory Burch sandals in her hand along with her iPod. Sandra's heart jumped a little at the site of the device.

"Do you have reception?" She asked as she picked up her step.

Belinda shook her head. "No, I want to take some pictures for my Facebook page and Instagram to post when we get out of here. Make all my sisters jelly."

"Oh, too bad." Sandra was visibly disappointed and suddenly found she was fighting off a panic attack.

You OK?" Belinda said, taking a step toward the older woman.

"Not really. I'm freaked out. I don't usually have anxiety, but maybe it's all the Xanax on this island that's making me nervous."

"Sure, that and two dead vixens."

"Well, yes, that could cause some apprehension."

Belinda dug her right foot into the sand.

"Do you think Laverne really killed herself now that Justine is dead?"

Sandra gazed across the beach, noticing all the empty beach chairs and umbrellas set up for a large group. Green, yellow and blue decorative pillows brightened up a solid tan couch which sat in the sand looking out into infinity.

"I don't know what to think," she said, starting to walk down the beach. Belinda scrambled to her feet.

"You know, back in the day, Laverne was a nice person. She had some tough breaks, losing her son to cancer when he was a little boy. Then she lost her breast to cancer when she was in her 40's," Sandra continued. "But I think she knew about her husband's infidelity with men. I think it made her bitter. The sun rose and set with that man as far as she was concerned."

"How about Justine? Damn, her face was nasty, that's for sure. It didn't look like a good way to go."

"No it did not," Sandra said, trying to get her former friend's face out of her mind.

The two women walked quietly on the beach for a few minutes.

"So, are you ever going to tell us about the accusation pointed at you?" Belinda asked.

Sandra stopped. She shrugged and then walked a few paces to a chair. She let herself relax a little into the seat. Belinda stood. Sandra looked up at the young woman, still dressed in her yoga outfit. Her dark hair was pulled back tight in a ponytail and she wore no makeup. "Are you wearing sunblock?" Sandra asked. "I sell a nice light foundation with a 30 SPF. I can sell it to you wholesale."

"Quit stalling," Belinda said, moving under an umbrella. "Who did the voice say you killed?"

Sandra smiled slightly. "Tina Van Steele. She was a novice with me at the convent. I really liked her. She was new and Mother Superior thought that having her room with me might help her ease into the day-to-day. She was so sweet and polite. Then I found out she was pregnant. She had already given one child up for adoption and this was her second pregnancy. She confided in me and wanted me to help her hide the obvious, but I was having none of that."

Belinda sat down and turned to Sandra. "What happened?"

"Of course I told Mother Superior right away. She was a slut living amongst us."

Belinda gulped. "Seriously, what happened to her?"

"They threw her out into the street, which is obviously where she belonged."

"Damn girl, you're bad ass."

Sandra sat up taller. "Yes, I believe I am."

"What did she do then? How did she die?"

"She jumped off the Golden Gate Bridge."

Belinda shivered. She stared at Sandra, trying to get a read on what was going on in her mind. Religious, self-righteous and condemning, is what she saw in the former nun's eyes.

"Did you feel responsible?"

Sandra laughed bitterly. "Of course not. I didn't get her pregnant. I didn't lie to get into the Covent. I had nothing to do with it."

"But you could have been a little nicer to her, maybe found a way she could leave and not be tossed out on her ass. You know, like decent human being?"

"Her own actions drove her to it," Sandra said sharply. "If she had not slept around and had some morals it wouldn't have happened."

She turned to Belinda and stared at her with hard, sanctimonious eyes, daring her to continue the conversation.

Belinda held the stare and then looked out into the ocean, realizing that the woman sitting next to her scared the shit out of her.

II

Mattie came into the dining room and saw Jerdie, her back to her, on the lanai. Audrey walked toward her and she stepped out of the way. They both smiled nervously at each other.

"Hey Jerdie, can I speak with you for a minute?" Mattie asked.

Jerdie jumped a little and turned.

"Sure, what's up?"

"Walk with me?"

"Alright," Jerdie said, looking around for Audrey. Then, figuring she could take care of herself, she followed Mattie's lead.

They walked outside and down a few steps and turned onto a path that wove through a grove of fig and green plum trees. They found a small bench overlooking the pool area and both sat down.

"What do you think is really going on?" Mattie asked.

Jerdie raised her perfectly waxed eyebrows.

"I don't know, you're the one declaring everyone dead!"

"Come on, you must have some sort of opinion."

Jerdie dug around in her 1940's-style white linen pants pocket and came up with a cigarette and lighter.

"Damn, I've been trying to smoke this all morning but I keep getting interrupted." She lit the cigarette and blew smoke into the air.

"You mind?" Mattie said, waving the smoke away.

"Oh, sorry." Jerdie stood up and walked a few feet away and turned to the vet. Mattie didn't look good. Her hair wasn't brushed and she was wearing some God-awful mom-jeans with a blouse made of cotton with dogs on it. She had on some makeup, but it looked like from the day before which gave her raccoon eyes.

Mattie spoke. "I can't be certain, but I think Laverne was murdered."

"Really?" Jerdie asked. "I mean, I guess it makes sense." She frowned. "Oh, hell no! We've got a murderer on this island!"

"We might, I don't want to freak everyone out, although they're probably coming up with the same conclusions."

"Let's be real," Jerdie said walking closer. "How was Laverne murdered?"

"Well, either Laverne brought the poison and she did in fact kill herself, or someone else did. My money's on someone else."

III

Jerdie took a deep breath.

"And Justine?"

"I still think she was smothered. Remember, she asked for a sleeping pill so she was out of it. Someone could have easily come into her room. She looked like she put up a fight—her nose was pretty bad off—but she was probably too groggy to really fight off her attacker. Being smothered by a pillow is so bizarre. Why not poison another vixen instead of making such a scene?"

They were both silent. Jerdie flung away her cigarette. Mattie frowned at her.

"Really?" Jerdie said.

Mattie shrugged. "Fine, litter the place, I don't care. I kind of hate it here."

"I know, right? But listen, maybe there's a clue in the poem that's in all of our rooms."

"I don't remember it. I've been a little busy declaring people dead."

"Sure," Jerdie said. "It goes:

Ten little vixens went out to drink wine; One choked her little self and then there were nine

Nine little Vixens gossiped until late; One overslept herself and then there were eight."

The two women grinned, happy for a moment that they solved the puzzle.

"It can't be a coincidence," Mattie said. "Laverne choked on a poisoned gin and tonic and Justine overslept because she was dead."

"And the murder has to be U.N Owen, as in 'one unknown loony lady at large."

"That has to be it," Jerdie said. "There's another person on this island!"

"I think we should get a few of the others and go looking for this mysterious person. It's better than sitting around waiting to get knocked off."

"You're right," Jerdie said. "I can be a badass if I try. I took an advanced self-defense course last year. I know where to kick someone where it will really hurt."

Mattie laughed. She didn't know why, but she felt better. Maybe she would sit on the beach for a few hours later or go for a swim. She really loved to swim.

CHAPTER TEN

I

The women knocked on Belinda's door.

"Enter," she yelled from the bathroom.

Jerdie and Mattie looked around the room, amazed at the amount of clothes and makeup that were scattered everywhere. Tiny thongs, bras, bathing suits and shorts were flung around the room with little or no thought.

"Did someone break in?" Mattie said, half-serious.

Belinda walked out in nothing but a thong and a sheer bra.

"I see nothing's changed, still an exhibitionist," Jerdie said looking away.

"Whatever," Belinda said. "Why are you here?"

The two women explained their theory as Belinda grabbed some clothes from the floor and stepped into the yoga outfit she had worn on the beach.

"That's like, crazy!" she said. "But how could anyone poison Laverne, she made all her drinks?"

"I know, but I was thinking at some point she had to have set her glass down," Mattie said. The other two were skeptical. "No really, she was getting some snacks and she went to the bathroom a few times. I think she was incontinent."

"Oh yeah, she used to tell us that when she sneezed, she peed a little, but I think it was a lot." Belinda said.

"Right, so maybe she set her glass down by an open window. I mean, the damn place is all open windows and someone could have slipped the poison into her glass."

Jerdie wasn't buying it. "With all of us here? How could we not see it?"

"Because we were too busy screaming at each other," Mattie said.

"That's true. We were all over the place, yelling and attacking each other. Hell, an elephant could have walked into the room but we were so wound-up we could have missed it."

"I would have seen an elephant I think," Belinda said, rolling her eyes.

"I was using it as an example," Jerdie sighed.

"I knew that," Belinda said, a little hurt. "So, I'm in, I'll help you look around the island, but I need some sort of weapon. Maybe a fireplace poker or something."

"Right, we do need some sort of protection," Mattie said.

"I brought a gun, just a little one," Jerdie said brightly. "I live in Sydney, so no customs. I bring it everywhere."

"That helps," Mattie said. "But we'll have to plan this a little better. We can't go running around with a fireplace poker and a toy gun, hoping to outwit some crazy-ass killer."

"Right," Belinda said, lying down on a recliner. "Let me know when everything's all planned out. I'm going to take a little nap. I don't know about you, but I didn't sleep very well last night."

II

After a lunch of mango salad and peach sorbet with berries, Belinda, Mattie, Jerdie and Audrey began searching the house. They started at the bottom of the Balinese-style mansion. They discovered 12 bedrooms and a sort of bunkhouse for what looked to be for live-in staff. They searched the bathrooms and the closets of the bedrooms and didn't find anything strange. There was a room filled with children's books and toys, along with four bunk beds. Cheerful wallpaper and a bathroom with a big tub with rubber ducks and other bath toys greeted them. They searched under the beds and again through the closets. They searched the gardens and walked a mile to the airport. They were excited to see a small control tower, but almost cried when they found all the wires cut into tiny pieces.

"Not even MacGyver could repair this mess," Audrey said.

"Who?" asked Jerdie smiling.

"Oh, stop," Audrey replied.

The scouts carefully walked the path along the cliffs, looking in the bushes. There were outbuildings full of sailing equipment, lawn mowers and a small tractor. They found some tools they took as weapons, but no murdering TV producer.

They finally circled back to the pool, where Cookie and Tracy were resting on large floaties in the blue water, a tall drink in each of their cup holders. Sandra sat on a chaise lounge under an umbrella, her face tighter than normal. The waves of the beach lapped only a few feet away, and Belinda felt she had done enough work for the day.

"I'm going to get into my bathing suit and join you," she said. "It's too hot to look for a murderer."

"A what?" Cookie asked, sitting up on her float and almost tipping herself into the pool.

"A killer is on the loose, ha-ha!" Belinda teased as she walked past. "We figured it out. U.N. Known is a murdering bitch. We need to find her and kill her before she gets us. Or get off the island. Anyone need a drink?"

All the women raised their hands.

III

"It's a good thing this place has as many bars as it does bathrooms," Mattie said, pouring wine into plastic wine glasses. "I don't think I've seen so much wine since we went to Jill's winery. Speaking of Jill, where is she?"

"Here I am," she said, sitting further down the beach, an umbrella hiding her.

Audrey jumped. "Jesus, you scared me."

"I saw you all searching the property. Did you find your killer?"

"They think Laverne and Justine were both murdered. By the person who invited us here," Cookie said. "They've been looking for signs that someone else is with us on this beautiful, yet deadly island. Dun, dun, dun dun!" She sang.

"Is that true?" Tracy said.

Jerdie explained their theory to the other women. Cookie snorted.

"You are ridiculous," Cookie said. "I don't believe a word of it. Laverne killed herself and I'm sure Justine killed herself too. She was a loser. She had plenty of reasons to do herself in."

"Wow, that's harsh," Tracy said.

Cookie turned to her best friend. "I'm sorry, was I speaking to you?"

Tracy stared at Cookie in defiance. "Never push a loyal person to the point where they don't give a damn," Tracy said, softly falling into the water and swimming to the edge.

"Well I for one am just going to wait it out in this luxurious house," Jill said. "I will miss Henry though, even if he won't talk to me."

"Do you blame him?" Audrey asked.

"No, but I loved him so much. That's why I did it."

The women looked at each other nervously.

"Did what exactly?"

"I killed Cherry on purpose. It's no use denying it now, not when we're all going to die on this rock. Damn, I did a good show of pretending to be insane, but I really did think I went a little crazy. It served her right, him too. But no regrets," Jill said, raising her glass of wine. "No regrets, my little vixens."

IV

Belinda and Mattie walked upstairs together. When they were out of earshot Belinda said, "What the hell was that all about?"

Mattie shook her head. "No clue, but Jill has definitely lost it. She's gone around the bend."

"Do you think she's the killer?" Belinda asked, stopping on the stairs and looking nervously down at the beach.

"I don't think so. I think she's lost her mind, but I doubt she's a killer. I mean, I doubt that she'd kill *us*...oh shit, I have no idea."

The two women arrived in the Great Room and looked down at vixens in the pool and on the beach. They gazed out to sea with its endless horizon, the sun shining hot on the water, and both quietly came to the same conclusion.

There was no one on the island except for eight vixens.

CHAPTER ELEVEN

I

"Fine, then we're wrong about the lunatic. We freaked each other out so much that we searched the damn island and found *nada*," Belinda said.

"And yet, we have two dead women, you can't deny that fact."

"Right, but couldn't they both be accidents or both be suicide?"

"I suppose Laverne's death could be, but what about poor Justine? Did she fall onto the pillow in her sleep and then get back into bed and die?" Mattie said.

"Well maybe the Ambien killed her. Maybe she was allergic to it or something and the killer knew that. Who gave it to her?"

"Jerdie gave it to her, but I doubt she killed her. Or did she? Hell,

I don't know anything anymore. We can't start turning on each other."

Belinda smirked. "Well we've done it before. We're really quite good at it."

"Good at what?" asked Audrey, walking into the room.

"Turning on each other," Mattie continued. "First we thought there was a crazy murdering TV producer running around the island, now we're back to thinking Laverne and Justine killed themselves..."

"But how could Justine...?"

"I don't know," Mattie yelled. "I fucking don't have an answer."

"Stop yelling!" Belinda shouted. "Bitch, you are freaking me out!"

They all took a deep breath.

"Whatcha doin?" Jerdie asked, quietly coming into the room.

They all jumped.

"Jesus, you scared me," Audrey said.

"Wow, you guys look like you saw a ghost."

"Ha-ha," Belinda said. "No, we're back to attacking and accusing one another."

Jerdie walked to the refrigerator and opened it. "Boring," she said. "Let's talk about something else. Anyone have a new topic?"

Cookie and Tracy walked into the room, neither one looking at each other.

"You need to get your life together, that's what you need to do," Cookie said. "If I were you I would tell your boss to give you a raise and part of the profits. That's what I would do. Tell them you'll walk if they don't. You're a decent comic, and more important, you're a woman comic. You don't have to be fantastic, just tell some funny jokes to the old people and you have a career. But ask for more money. Take my advice. I'm always right."

"That's what you think," Tracy said. "You always have advice for everyone. Maybe you should take your own advice and get a life."

"What the hell did you say to me?"

"You heard me. All you do is shop and entertain Kurt's clients. You're a trophy wife who's getting old. How much plastic surgery can you have before your face melts and you finally eat something and gain a few pounds and your husband replaces you? Your kids don't talk to you and I'm your only real friend. But you're pushing me on that one."

"What in the hell came over you?" Cookie asked, wide-eyed.

"I don't know, but it feels good. I'm coming to my senses I guess. It occurred to me that I only exist when you need something."

"That's not true," Cookie said softly.

"Ladies, ladies, another time, OK?" Audrey said.

"Fine," said Tracy, "But we're not through here. I've got a lot more to…"

"Wait, someone's running up the stairs," Mattie said, her voice shaking.

They could see a person running toward them, but the sun blocked her out. Who was it?

Sandra finally appeared and they all knew.

"Jill?" whispered Mattie.

"Dead," screeched the usually calm Sandra. "She's Goddamned dead."

Seven vixens looked at each other. For once, no one said a word.

II

A udrey could smell the rain coming. She looked at the sky and saw the clouds turning as dark as the night. The lights lit up the path and the stairs, but the night was still black. Jerdie, Mattie and Tracy were bringing up Jill's body and she walked down to give them a hand. Cookie and Belinda watched from the terrace and Sandra sat in the dining room, nursing a shot of tequila Belinda had poured her.

There was a sudden clap of lightning and the rain started to pour out of the sky.

As the women carrying the body picked up their step, Belinda walked into the dining room. Sandra, shell-shocked, had hardly touched her drink. She stared at Belinda, whose eyes questioned hers.

"So…?"

"Yes, it happened again," Sandra laughed bitterly, pointing at the glasses. "Look for yourself. There are only seven."

III

J ill had been placed on her bed like the other dead vixens. Mattie closed the windows and door and shut it softly. "Poor Jill," she said. She came downstairs to join the others in the Great Room. Cookie was washing dishes and putting out some cheese and crackers. Jerdie was looking out at the rain through the open French doors as the trees lurched in the wind and were attacked by the rain. Belinda and Audrey were sitting on the couch, staring off into space. Sandra was still at the table, staring at the vixen wine glasses. Tracy was writing in a notebook.

Mattie was pale. "Well, I doubt she was poisoned because somebody smacked the shit out of her head."

"Are you sure she didn't have a heart attack or something? People die all the time in saunas," Audrey said.

"I suppose she could have fainted and hit her head, but she wasn't on the floor. If that's the case, someone had to go back in and pick her up." Mattie said quietly. "But she could have died because of the heat. People do all the time. Combined with the drop in blood pressure, dehydration and severe heat exhaustion, people usually pass out. In a sauna, that can lead to serious burns when the skin comes in contact with hot surfaces. There are a few burns on her legs."

"Maybe she had a heart attack from the heat and stress," Belinda said.

"That might have caused her blood pressure to spike," Mattie said. "When your body temperature rises, you get light headed and your thinking gets all screwed up. For lack of a better term, she could very well have cooked her brain."

"Maybe someone locked her in and then came and sat her back up," Sandra said. "What do you think?"

"Jesus Christ, do I look like Sherlock Holmes? I'm a veterinarian! Not a doctor, not a detective, but a veterinarian!"

"And a damn good one," Audrey said, as she stood and walked toward Mattie. She gave her a hug.

"God, I am so tired of pronouncing vixens dead." She began to cry.

The others looked at each other and Belinda came up to hug her.

Cookie stayed in the kitchen, drinking her wine and watching.

"This is all sweetness and unicorns, but we have a very big problem, namely someone is killing vixens. I want to know who the hell it is," she said. "We need to figure out a way to stay alive. Does anyone have a clue?" Cookie looked at each of the remaining women. "Anyone?" she asked frantically. Her forehead actually moved.

"There's no one else on the island, we looked everywhere," Jerdie said.

Audrey stepped back and surveyed the room.

"I think you're right about that," she said softly. "Although I have a theory. I am starting to believe that Ms. Owen is on the island. She knew all about us and how to convince us through flattery to get us to come to this island for an obvious fake reality TV show. There are no signs of anyone else living here and we haven't seen a boat or a plane while we've been here, so there's only one explanation on how she came onto the island." She paused. All eyes were on her, waiting for her to say it.

"It's right in front of you—don't you see? Ms. Owen is one of us."

IV

"I hate you all," Belinda yelled. "You're all mean and horrible and one of you is a killer. I hate you, I hate you!"

"Calm the hell down," screamed Jerdie. "Get a grip!"

Audrey looked over at Belinda and whispered. "It's OK, It's ok." She turned to the others and continued. "Don't you see, it just makes sense that U.N. Owen is one of us," she said. "I don't see any other explanation, do you?"

She stared at Cookie, who turned away.

"Of the 10 vixens that came to the island, three are in the clear. They're also dead, but they're not suspects. There are seven vixens left and one is a murdering bitch."

She paused and looked around. "Do you agree, or do you have another theory? Because I, for one, would rather be wrong."

No one said a word.

"So you agree with me then. Shit, I was hoping I was wrong."

"It's unthinkable, but I guess you're right," Tracy, said looking at the floor.

"I absolutely agree," Belinda said, "And I have a strong opinion about who it..."

Audrey put up her hand to stop her.

"We'll figure that out, but let's not start accusing everyone and anyone. We need the facts."

"One of you is possessed by the devil," Sandra said, rubbing her fingers nervously on the gold cross around her neck.

"I can't believe it," Tracy whispered.

"Now here's what I know for sure..."Audrey started.

"Hey Oprah, who put you in charge?" Cookie said, stepping forward. "You always take over and boss everyone around with your facts and quotes. You talk too much. You know too much. Maybe you're the killer."

Audrey shrugged her shoulders and stepped aside. "Fine Cookie, you take the lead on this. What information or facts do you have that would point to a killer vixen?"

Cookie thought a minute and slugged back her wine. "I don't know, but maybe I'll lock myself in my room until you're all dead and I'm the last one standing."

"We're not really on a reality show, Cookie. This is life or death shit," Tracy said.

Cookie turned to her friend and gave her a withering look. "Yes

Tracy, I know I am not on a show. Jesus, what crawled up your ass today?"

Tracy looked at her with astonishment. "Are you kidding? People are dying. Our friends are being murdered."

"These people are not my friends," Cookie said as she stared into her empty wine glass. "They used to be my friends. Then they screwed me over at some point. They're all losers anyway. Who cares about Jill or Laverne or Justine? Those friendships were based on booze and using each other. They were fake friendships."

"Whoa, very empathetic as usual," Tracy said. "You can be such a bitch Cookie."

"Because I'm telling the truth that makes me a bitch?"

"No, because you've always been a bitch. Especially to me. But that's over. I'm done with you. You always push me. I swear, it's like you want me to hate you."

Cookie stared at her long-time friend and then burst out laughing. "What, you're breaking up with me? Are you going to kill me too?"

Tracy shook her head and turned her back.

"Well then, anyone else have anything to say to me?" Cookie said, still chuckling. The other women looked away, except Audrey who held back a smirk.

"So who could it be," Cookie said, walking to the bar to pour more chardonnay. "Laverne was poisoned so anyone could have done it. Mattie, you can get drugs at work and Jerdie and Belinda, not to be racist, but.... you know people, so you can get drugs easier than anybody."

"Did you just fucking disrespect me?" Jerdie, said, jumping to her feet.

"What did you say about me *coño*?" Belinda said, joining the trio.

"Well excuse, me but your language proves that neither of you are that far from being all ghetto."

"You need to quit acting like you're so damn perfect. All bitches have glitches," Belinda replied, stepping closer.

Cookie smiled at the others as if to say, 'See what I mean?'

"Oh darling, go buy a personality," she said.

Sandra broke in: "To think that I—a woman who took her vows with Christ—could kill another human being is completely ridiculous," she said. "I was married to God."

"And then you divorced him," Jerdie said. "Get over yourself. We're all under suspicion."

"Whoever it is really hates all of us," Audrey said. The women looked at her. "Ahh, of course, I broke up the fabulous Ladies who Lunch," she said. "That's fair. But, I also walked away because I was so sick and tired of your shallowness and your stupidity. Jesus, you don't kill someone because they're stupid. You just move away and get a fabulous job and new friends. Done deal. But, OK, let's agree that we're all suspects, that Unknown is one of us. So let's start by looking at the facts and ask questions."

She walked to a drawer in a nearby credenza and found a pad of paper and a pen. She returned to the dining table. One by one the vixens sat down.

Audrey drew some lines down the page and put everyone's name at the top.

"First question. Is there anyone here who could not, by some weird reason, not have poisoned Laverne or smothered Justine or ...somehow killed Jill in a sauna? Seriously, that's a weird way to die."

Everyone looked at each other.

"Well," said Tracy, "I hate to say it, but Mattie does have access to drugs and knows how much it would take to kill someone."

Mattie jumped up from her chair. "Oh my God, now you Tracy?" She was trembling. "I couldn't do that, I took an oath."

"Veterinarians don't take a Hippocratic oath, do they?" Jerdie asked Audrey, who shrugged her shoulders.

"Being admitted to the profession of veterinary medicine, I solemnly swear to use my scientific knowledge and skills for the benefit of society through the protection of animal health and welfare, the prevention and relief of animal suffering, the conservation of animal resources, the promotion of public health, and the advancement of medical knowledge," Mattie recited.

"Great, fine, we believe you," Cookie said.

Mattie wasn't finished "I will practice my profession conscientiously, with dignity, and in keeping with the principles of veterinary medical ethics."

"Oh, do shut up," Cookie added.

"I accept as a lifelong obligation the continual improvement of my professional knowledge and competence."

Cookie glared at Mattie. "You done?"

"Yes, I'm done," she said, with tears in her eyes. "And in case you weren't listening, that's not what Audrey asked us."

Audrey nodded her head.

"Right, what I said was is there anyone who could not possibly have committed any of the murders, but I think that's a big no. We're all suspects."

The vixens took that in.

V

"**S**o one of us is a killer," Belinda said. "Wow."

"I can't believe it," Tracy said. "That's about as hateful as you can get."

"Now let's look at the evidence," Audrey said. "Does anyone have any proof that one of us might be a suspect?"

Belinda looked at Cookie. "Well, Jerdie has a gun."

The others stared at her.

Jerdie smiled. "Oh please, no one's been shot. I carry a small gun for protection. I'm kind of rich you know? I go out a lot and I'll be damned if I'm going to let someone take advantage of me."

"How do you own a gun in Australia?" asked Audrey.

Jerdie shrugged. "You can have anything you want when you have money."

The other nodded their heads.

"Any other weapons?" Audrey queried. No one spoke.

"Any chance you can get the gun and show us and lock it up somewhere?"

All eyes were on Jerdie. "Sure, whatever."

The vixens waited.

"Now?"

"I think it would make us feel better, "Audrey replied.

"Fine," she said standing up and walking to her room. "But don't talk about me while I'm gone like you used to."

The women stared at their nails and at the paintings of Tahitian women on the walls, which they all suspected were original Gauguin's.

"Hey, all this death is making me hungry. Anyone want something more to eat?" Tracy asked, not waiting for an answer. She got up from the table and walked into the kitchen, where the women could still see her. She opened the refrigerator and stared.

"This fruit needs to be eaten or it will go bad. It's not fattening." She grabbed items out of the huge refrigerator and pulled a large platter from the cupboard. At the same time that Jerdie walked downstairs with her gun, Tracy walked back into the dining room with cheese, sliced papaya, kiwi and passion fruit on a platter and set in on the coffee table.

Jerdie walked over to Audrey and sat down next to her. She set a pink leather purse on the table, unzipped an outside pocket and pulled out a small handgun.

Cookie laughed. "That's a gun?"

The weapon had a pink handle and looked like a toy.

"It's a real gun, "Jerdie assured her. "It's a Rugger LCP and it fits in my purse and my bra. I learned to shoot two bullets in the chest and then one in the face in my self-defense class, so I feel pretty confident when I'm carrying."

Jerdie pulled the slide and removed the magazine and showed the empty chamber to everyone.

"Now what? We don't have a safe."

"How about we throw it into the ocean?" Cookie said.

"What the eff?"

"Really, you can't buy a new one since you're so damn rich?"

Jerdie sighed. "Fine. Whatever. Let's do it."

The women stood up. "I need a glass of wine," Cookie said.

"Me too," the rest of the vixens chimed in.

"Let's do a selfie when we're down there," Cookie said. "Once we get out of here we can sell it to *People Magazine* when they write our story."

VI

The vixens quickly walked past the pool area, avoiding the path to the sauna, and wandered through the tennis court. They stood on the sand staring out at the tide.

"Wow, that's a hell of a tide," Audrey said. She gazed at the beach that was now carpeted with tiny, perfect pastel shells of all varieties.

"I guess I need to walk out there and throw the hell out of this gun or it'll wash back up on shore," Jerdie said. She rolled up her white linen pants, adjusted her peach off-the-shoulder top and kicked off her Tory Burch flip-flops. It seemed as if she was walking a mile to the water's edge and the sand was as hard as concrete. She finally felt the water lapping over her toes—which she noticed were in a serious need of a pedicure. She waded farther in.

"Hey, it's not too cold," she yelled to the vixens who were watching her every move. She moved further out to where the water was splashing at her knees. Small waves slapped her legs and she fought to stay upright. She pulled her gun purse over her shoulder and over her head and started to swing it over her head like a slingshot. Finally, she let go. The gun sailed through the sky and landed in the water about 70 yards out with a loud splash. The vixens on the beach applauded.

Jerdie turned around and bowed to the women. She was immediately knocked into the water by a wave that hit her from behind.

"Shit," she yelled when she came up soaking wet.

Tracy tossed her shoes, pulled up her floral lace shift dress and ran into the ocean.

"Are you OK?"

Jerdie laughed. "I'm fine, and this water is very refreshing. I think it took the edge off."

"Sure, that and you tossing your gun in the ocean, that works for me," Tracy said splashing water on her face and armpits.

"Ahh, I love the ocean," Jerdie said.

"Really? I didn't think black people could swim."

Jerdie stopped splashing and stared at Tracy.

Tracy laughed. "Ha, just fucking with ya."

Jerdie threw her head back and laughed, and then splashed Tracy, who splashed back.

Belinda, Audrey, Sandra and Cookie stood on the shore and watched the antics. Cookie glanced over and noticed Belinda stripping off her clothes. She scowled.

"I bet you thought all the Mexicans went in the ocean with their clothes on," Belinda said as she took off her thong. "Lighten up

Cookie. You could wake up dead tomorrow."

Audrey watched the naked young woman go and decided to take off her Tommy Bahama dress. She tossed it to Sandra and ran off to join the others, wearing nothing but her bra and underpants.

"Last one in is a dead vixen," she yelled over her shoulder, laughing.

Cookie and Sandra looked at each other.

"I'm fine here," Cookie said.

"Ditto," said Sandra.

They both sat down on the sand, watching the screaming vixens splash and swim in the Pacific Ocean as the sun sat high in the sky. A lone seagull flew overhead.

VII

B elinda and Audrey strolled into the kitchen after showering and changing. Belinda wore a tiny navy blue halter-top and a high-waisted gauze skirt, her tan and tight stomach showing. She was barefoot and sauntered in, declaring, "I'm starving. And I'm hungry for seafood. Do we have any fish?"

Audrey moved to the freezer and opened it. "Yep. We have prawns, crabs and lobster. If we start defrosting now we can eat by nine."

Belinda thought a moment. "Sounds good, I'll make a pitcher of martinis, just to mix things up a bit, and you can start dinner."

"What's for dinner? Who's cooking it?" asked Cookie as she entered the kitchen wearing a green tropical print maxi dress and sparkly flip-flops.

"We've got shellfish. Is there anything you want to make?" replied Audrey.

Cookie put her head in the fridge and came out with some cucumbers. "I can do a lot with these." she said, laughing. Audrey and Belinda exchanged glances and then burst out laughing.

"I still got it," Cookie said, kicking up her leg.

As Cookie searched for more ingredients and grabbed bowls and a knife, the other women filed in.

Mattie was dressed in boyfriend jeans and a white peasant blouse trimmed in mint. She was also barefoot; her hair was wet and piled on top of her head.

"Look at this scene," she said and then stopped. *No use jinxing it*, she thought. "What are we making?"

"Seafood, and I'm making cucumber pickles. I don't know why, but it sounds yummy," Cookie said.

Mattie looked at the ex-beauty queen and noticed that, through the plastic surgery and Botox, she was still a beautiful woman. Her green eyes sparkled and her cheekbones were still sharp as ever.

"I think this calls for something special. I'm kind of over wine tonight," Mattie said.

"I'm already on it," Belinda yelled as she waved the empty bottle of Grey Goose in the air. "Ice cold martinis for all!"

"Martoonis , woop, woop," Cookie yelled.

The rest of the evening, the vixens chopped and sliced and diced. They boiled and broiled and pickled. They set the table with the Wedgewood china from the cupboard set with blue hibiscus and a gold border. They drank their martinis, and then drank another. They had collectively created a seafood banquet. A platter was piled high with steamed crab, lobster and prawns to be served with mustard sauce, anchovy butter and dill mayonnaise. Cookie had made cucumber pickles with cinnamon and cloves, and Jerdie put a potato salad together with baby potatoes she found in the walk-in pantry while Sandra served a beetroot salad.

The vixens sat down at the table and stared at the feast they had created.

"Wow, this is awesome," Belinda said. "Who would have guessed we did this without, you know, killing each other?"

The others nodded and smiled.

"A toast," Audrey said, holding up her glass. "To the deceased vixens. May they be drinking vodka in heaven."

The others held their glasses up.

"But hell is more likely," Cookie laughed.

"To the vixens!"

"You know, this is just like that trip we took to Jill's vineyard that summer," Sandra said, picking up a crab leg. "I actually had fun on that trip. Remember the Beach Boys concert and the spa?"

"Oh my God, the spa was to die for," Belinda said giggling. "The mud bath was fantastic. Remember the old tubs and that lady named...what was her name?"

"Helga!" Audrey and Cookie said at the same time.

"That's right. Holy shit, she was like a Nazi or something. Remember? She told us to strip naked and then get in those old time bathtubs like in the Viagra commercial."

"Right, except Sandra wore her underwear," Mattie said.

Sandra shrugged and took a sip of her martini.

"Oh, and then we sank into the mud for an hour. I thought I was going to get clusterphobia," Belinda said.

"What?" Jerdie asked. "You mean claustrophobia?"

"Yeah, that."

The women all laughed.

"So, then we all had to get out and she hosed us down with a fucking garden hose!" Belinda said. "It was so old school—I loved it."

The others nodded and reminisced. They laughed and cracked crab and drank another round of martinis.

"I miss some of those days," Jerdie said. "It was so good for a while. Fun, you know? What happened?"

Everyone grew quiet.

"Sorry, I didn't mean to kill the mood. I was just wondering, not blaming anyone. We all started to turn into assholes I guess."

"Speak for yourself," said Cookie, her eyes squinting. "I was always the same person."

"You're right," Audrey said. "You were always an asshole."

Tracy spit her drink back into the glass. "Hang on, let's not keep this going. I have a joke."

The women groaned.

"No, come on, let's keep the good juju going. I'm actually enjoying myself."

"Fine, tell us the joke," Cookie said smiling at her friend.

"Right. A large woman wearing a sleeveless sundress walks into a bar in Dublin," she began.

"She raises her right arm, revealing a huge, hairy armpit and, as she points to all the people sitting at the bar she asks, "What man here will buy a lady a drink?" The bar goes silent as the patrons try to ignore her. But down at the end of the bar, an owley-eyed drunk slams his hand down on the counter and bellows, "Give the ballerina a drink!" The bartender pours the drink and the woman chugs it down. She turns to the patrons and again points around at all of them, revealing the same hairy armpit, and asks, "What man here will buy a lady a drink?" Once again, the same little drunk slaps his money down on the bar and says, "Give the ballerina another drink!" The bartender approaches the little drunk and says, "Tell me, Paddy, it's your business if you want to buy the lady a drink, but why do you keep calling her the ballerina?" The drunk replies, "Any woman who can lift her leg that high has got to be a ballerina!"

The women laughed hysterically and pounded the table. Belinda and Audrey lifted their legs, and Mattie looked under her arms while Cookie wiped tears from her eyes as the women fought to forget the women upstairs.

CHAPTER TWELVE

Laverne — Dead
Justine — Dead
Jill — Dead

I

"**I** think we need to talk about the murders," Jerdie said as she drained her glass. "This is all fun and games right now and it's really great that we're having a decent time and reminiscing, but more than likely, someone at this table has killed three of our, umm, friends. That's freaking me out. Can we talk about it?"

She watched her fellow vixens carefully.

"Fine, let's do this," Tracy said. "Audrey, can you lead this discussion?"

"What? Again? Why her?" Cookie said raising her voice. "Why is she always the go-to-person?"

"Well Cookie, it makes sense because she's on a TV show where she talks about murders and sometimes even solves the murders. She's like a vixen detective," replied Tracy.

"It's a TV show!"

"I know it's a TV show," Tracy said firmly. "But she still has the experience. Do you want to do it?"

"Actually I do," Cookie said. "Where's the notebook and the pen?"

All the women stared at Cookie. No one moved until Audrey stood up and retrieved the notebook she had been writing in and handed it to the beauty queen vixen.

"Here you go," Audrey said kindly.

"OK then. Fine. Let's do this. Belinda, where were you when Jill died and did you hate her enough to kill her like you killed your business partner?"

Belinda's head shot up. "What the fuck?"

"I asked you a question," Cookie said as she stared Belinda down. "Did you kill her because she didn't tell you her company was going public? I know you have a Latin temper and it can go off. I've seen it happen. Like that time we were at the James Taylor concert and those people kept talking and you finally walked down and got in the woman's face and you acted all ghetto and told her you would cut her if she didn't shut the hell up? Remember that?"

Belinda's mouth fell open.

"Actually, if I remember correctly, Belinda is the one who finally got up and went to get security and the people were tossed out," Audrey said. "She didn't say a word while we were all passive aggressive and saying, 'shhhh' about one hundred times."

"Wow Cookie, your memory is fucked up. Do you think you might be crazy like your mother?" Jerdie said.

Cookie stared hard at Jerdie. That comment was a low blow, but she held her tongue. Everyone had heard Cookie complain about her mother, Veronica, in the past. How growing up with her bipolar mother was the stuff of nightmares: full of instability, violence and a sense of helplessness that was only relieved when Veronica would leave for weeks at a time to supposedly visit an ashram. Veronica had been dead for a decade, but Cookie still had the scars and she was sure that her mother had no idea that she was bipolar. In fact, the only thing Veronica was willing to admit was to having a temper problem. Fortunately for Cookie, after a lifetime of struggling with the mind games, the pathological lying, the constant conflict Veronica created by pitting she and her brothers against each other, her parents divorced and her father gained full custody. Cookie could finally breathe again, but she always worried that she also had a mental illness; she had been seeing a shrink for more than a decade. So far, there was no diagnosis that she was bipolar; she was just a bitch, plain and simple.

"Seriously? You're bringing my mom into this?" She shook her head in disgust. "Jerdie, let's get real. Did you kill Justine? I think she made a pass at you once and you told her over your dead body."

The other women traded glances.

"What does that mean?" Jerdie asked. "Because it sounds like I am saying only if I died would I sleep with her. And she didn't really. We were both drunk and dancing and it got weird. Like college weird, you know? Nothing happened and I was just as much to blame as she was. I felt bad later, like I led her on."

"Did you kill her?" Cookie said, writing furiously in the notebook.

"Hell to the no!"

"Is that black talk?"

Jerdie looked at the other women.

"Are you kidding me with this shit? Someone take that notebook away from her or there's going to be a killing right here at this table."

Tracy reached her hand out to Cookie. "We don't think you have the skills to conduct this investigation," she said. "Nothing personal, but you don't have any tact. Give me the book."

"No."

"Really? Give me the book, Cookie. We don't want you to do this. Audrey is better suited for this kind of thing."

"Because she's on TV? "Cookie said, her voice rising.

"Yes, exactly. Get over it and give me the book," Tracy said firmly.

"Why are you so bossy all of a sudden?" She asked her friend.

Tracy thought a moment. "Because it's time. If something

happens to me tonight, or tomorrow or next week, I don't want to be known as your shadow, your whipping girl, your bitch. I want people to know that I stood up to you and frankly, I don't like you that much. You're mean to me. You're mean to everyone. I know it comes from insecurity from your mother issues, but I am tired of taking your shit. It stops here tonight. So give me the motherfucking notebook and shut the hell up."

Cookie was stunned, but she slid the book to Tracy, who then handed it to Audrey.

II

"Alrighty then," Audrey said, trying to lighten the mood. "Cookie is right that we have to ask some, umm, serious questions. And she's right that we more than likely—and I really hate to say it—but we have a murderer sitting at this table."

Cookie smiled. "See? That's what I said."

"Yes, you sure did," Audrey replied. "The question is, who would want to kill us and why?"

No one spoke.

"Let's put down some facts and hash this out. I doubt we're going to get a confession, but let's give this a go."

"OK, we already figured out that someone put poison in Laverne's gin and tonic, but the question is how? Audrey said. "We already know she was a pain in everyone's ass—although not enough to murder her—but maybe she really annoyed the killer. Does anyone have any ideas?"

Silence.

"Belinda, you were downstairs with her before anyone else arrived, is that true?"

Belinda scrunched her forehead, but nothing happened. "Sure, I guess I was, but that doesn't..."

"No, just a question, let's not get defensive just yet. Did Laverne open a new bottle or was it already open?"

"It was a new bottle I think. Yes, it was, because she was excited that it was Tanqueray, her favorite, as we all know. She said something like, 'a whole handle of Tanqueray, just for me?' You know how happy gin made her."

The others nodded and a few smiled.

"So if she opened the Tanqueray, it couldn't be tampered with and we all saw that Audrey tasted it from the bottle," Belinda said.

"Did anyone see her walk away from her drink for any length of time?"

Jerdie laughed. "Are you kidding? Laverne held onto her drinks as if her, umm, life depended on it. Jesus, that sounded terrible, but you know what I mean."

"We know what you mean," Tracy said.

Audrey wrote some notes and then said, "Let's move on to Justine, because that one truly looks like a murder, not a suicide. There is a remote possibility that Laverne killed herself. I don't see it, but it's possible." She thought for a moment. "Jerdie, where did you get the Ambien from?"

178

"My doctor prescribed it and I got it at my Costco pharmacy. I have plenty left but I'm not going to take it."

"Good, save it for the cops or whoever rescues us. It could have been something else that she took, of course."

"Like I said, you could have given her something bad, like an illegal drug," Cookie said. "You're in the pill business."

Jerdie took a deep breath. "I am in the vitamin business, you twat. Natural vitamins."

"Same thing," Cookie mumbled.

"I'm sure the Ambien was just fine, it's the death by pillow that freaks me out," Audrey said.

"And has anyone else seen a pillow like that around here? I know I haven't. Anyway, who found Justine?"

"Belinda and I found her," Mattie said uncomfortably. "You sent us up there to look for her because she was still sleeping."

"We thought she had a blanket pulled up over her face but it was that nasty pillow," Belinda said.

"Then you all came up and we looked at her face. We didn't touch anything until everyone was in the room."

"And from your medical training, you think she was smothered by the pillow, right Mattie?"

She nodded her head. "Right. I mean, I'm no CSI guy, but I've seen a few animals that have been smothered. Her eyes were blood red and there was bruising around her nose like someone was smashing it, so yes, that's my professional medical answer."

"So is anyone here too weak to have smothered Justine—who was obviously drugged or weakened by the Ambien—to have killed her with the pillow?"

No one said a word.

"Right, so it could have been any of us who snuck in during the night to kill here." said Audrey. "Great, we're not exactly getting anywhere are we?"

"So much for the TV Detective," snickered Cookie.

"Shall we move on to Jill?"

"Fine," Cookie said. "She either, had a heart attack from the heat and hit her head then got back up and sat on the bench and died, or someone snuck in and hit her in the head and she died while steaming. Like the lobster we just ate."

"Oh that's nice," Sandra said. "Very respectful of Jill."

"Oh hell, Jill confessed to murdering her husband," said Cookie. "If anyone is a murderer it's Jill. Crazy, nut job Jill."

"She was a little loony at the end," Belinda said. "She said she wanted to stay here."

"Lucky her, she got her wish," Tracy said, looking at the women's faces. "Too soon?"

"Do you think she might have killed herself too?" Sandra said.

"Could she have taken something as well, fallen, then stood back up and then died? I know people have died while sitting in saunas. Their hearts give out. Or something happens to their brains. But in the end, they die. Could that have happened?"

"Could all of the dead vixens have killed themselves you mean?"

Sandra nodded her head.

"Hmmm, anyone think that might be the case?"

The women mulled it over. Then Jerdie spoke up.

"As much as I would like to think there's some sort of suicide pact going on and knowing I'm not about to kill myself, that would be my preferred scenario, but it's not bloody likely."

"Jill didn't kill herself," Mattie said. "That wound on her head was what knocked her out and made her body go into shock. Then either the heat did her in, or the blow killed her outright."

Audrey wrote in the notebook again. "So Jill is a definite murder, Justine was most likely murdered and Laverne is 50/50. Does everyone agree?"

Six vixens nodded yes.

"While this doesn't solve anything, what we do know is that one of us is dangerous and a murderer," Audrey said. "We don't have any evidence pointing to any one of us, but we can be assured that it's true. What we now need to do is continue to look for a way out of this damn paradise and in the meantime be aware of danger. If you have any suggestions on how we can do this, I think we're all open to ideas. With that in mind, I also suggest we work together as a team. Whoever the killer is, we can't be easy targets. We know there is a crazy person among us. Don't take any risks, stay with a buddy, but be suspicious of everyone. We are all suspects. We could all be the killer."

She took a deep breath and stood up.

"That's all I've got. So with that, I'm going to go to my room, lock my door and going to sleep."

CHAPTER THIRTEEN

———

I

"I'm not sure what to think," Tracy said to Sandra as they sat outside on the patio by the pool. A small fire hissed in the gas fire pit as the waves gently lapped on the nearby shore.

"I know we've had our difference—big differences—but to think that someone we know is killing us in cold blood is beyond incredible."

"I know what you mean," Sandra said. "It makes perfect sense that it has to be one of us, but it seems so crazy, so unthinkable."

Tracy crossed her arms over her chest and shivered.

"I've seen a few people die and I think I know a suicide from a murder," she said. "There's no question, all three vixens were murdered."

"It seems like a bad dream," Sandra added. "I wish I could wake up and find myself back in my condo in California. I wish I'd never come here, but I thought I had an opportunity to make some money and finally get my company off the ground."

"It's a nightmare alright, but we have to keep on our toes. We have to be aware of our surroundings and of our fellow vixens."

"So…who do you think it is?" Sandra said, lowering her voice.

"You mean not counting us?" said Tracy. She grinned.

Sandra looked at Tracy hard and said, "Well, I know it's not me, so you can rest easy when you hang out with me."

"That's very reassuring," Tracy said. "And back at ya. I don't have it in me. I make people laugh, I don't kill them. So we can eliminate ourselves and try and figure out which of the other vixens is the killer."

They both sat in silence for a moment and then Tracy spoke. "If I was going to pick someone, with no facts to back me, I would say the killer is Audrey.

"Really?" Sandra looked out at the dark ocean, the stars hiding behind the clouds. "Why?"

"No real reason other than she got pissed and left us, back in the day. She pretty much told us we were backstabbing bitches and she was tired of hanging out with us. Then she wrote that article or whatever it was calling us out. By the way, some of it was right on the money. It was exhausting sometimes listening to Jill talk about her money and her right wing politics. And Cookie, yes, she can be a real bitch and she has a hard-on for Audrey for some reason after all those years of being friends. Then Audrey got that TV show where she is an investigative journalist, but on the show she seems to be a little more judgmental that she should be for a reporter."

"I think that's her TV personality," Sandra said, "I'm not sure I buy it though."

"Really? Do you have a vixen suspect in mind?"

"Mattie," Sandra said sternly.

"Really? I had her last on my list."

Sandra shook her head.

"No, don't you see. Two of the deaths were poison, and she does have a supply of lethal drugs on hand at the animal hospital," she said. "And she keeps pronouncing them dead. She's the only one here with medical knowledge and we're all looking at her for guidance when someone turns up dead. I think it's her and I advise you to watch out for her as well."

II

C ookie was in the kitchen with Jerdie, wiping down the counters again with vigor.

"I want to know who it is and when we're going to catch her," she said. "This is bullshit. I want to catch the murdering bitch and get off this rock and go home."

"I hear you," Jerdie said, "That's the million dollar question, isn't it? "

"But I want the answer now. We need to catch her and put her in a cage or tie her up or maybe even kill her. It would be self- defense."

Jerdie nodded her head slowly.

"I might have an idea, but I can't be sure. I might be wrong and then it would blow up in my face. But I'll keep thinking and get back to you."

"This is seriously freaking me out, I tell you. I'll run out of Xanax before we figure out who it is and stop her. I might have a nervous breakdown. You don't want to be around me when that happens."

Jerdie looked Cookie in the eye. "I don't exactly want to be around you normally, so yeah, we'd better figure this out before you lose your shit."

III

Mattie started pacing her room, tossing clothes and dumping out her purse.

"I have to get out of here. I am going crazy with all these dead vixens in the house, not to mention I am living under the same roof as a fucking crazy murderer."

"Isn't it murderess or is that an old timey thing?" Belinda asked.

"Are you serious?" Mattie said giving Belinda the stink-eye. "Who cares what we call her, she is crazy and she's quite literally killing us."

"I know, I'm not an idiot," Belinda said. "But we have to be ready and prepared at all times for something to happen. We can't turn our backs on anyone. The killer will make a mistake and there are six of us and only one of her. I know karate, so I can protect myself."

She demonstrated some karate moves, kicked into the air and screamed, "Back off!" Belinda pushed her hair out of her face and stared at Mattie, who was holding back laughter. "When I was fresh out of cooking school I got a job at a small upscale restaurant in Los Angeles, a very famous one, and I was so young and stupid," Belinda explained. "One day the chef—again, very famous—called me into the walk-in refrigerator to yell at me about some poultry I cut up wrong. When I turned to look at the damn chickens, he attacked me. He raped me in the fucking refrigerator, if you can believe it. After he was done, he yelled at me about the chicken and then walked out. I was so humiliated, but what could I do? He was my boss. No one would have believed me. His word against mine. I would have been blackballed right out of the gate. I decided to take karate lessons, so if he came at me I could defend myself. A few months later he surprised me in the produce room. I only had my yellow belt by then, but it was enough to break one of his fingers. He was too embarrassed to tell anyone how it broke. He knew it would be proof if I decided to file a lawsuit. What it did was empower me to start dreaming about my own restaurant. Eventually that dream came true and I became a black belt. I can kick ass."

"Good for you," Mattie said, clenching her fists. "But what about the rest of us? Somehow, the killer is surprising the vixens, and that's scaring the shit out of me. I don't know about you, but I don't want to die. Not even on an island paradise."

"But don't you see?" Belinda said. "We know she's going to make a move on one of us at some point, so we'll be ready. I can make a karate move and you can hit her with a frying pan or something."

"But if we don't know who it is, how can we prepare? It will drive us all crazy and we'll be walking on eggshells every second of the day."

Belinda sat on the floor and stretched, then stood up and bent into a cobra pose.

"Oh, I think I have an idea who it is," she said calmly, breathing out of her mouth.

"You know who it is? You know the killer vixen? Who is it?" Asked Mattie

Belinda stretched again and then bent down into a downward facing dog. "I don't have any evidence really, it's just a gut feeling. I'm a little bit psychic. My grandmother, I called her *Mamita*, had 'IT' too. We can kind of predict things and can see into the future sometimes. Once, *Mamita* had a dream about a man stalking my mom. She told this to my mother and my mother didn't believe it. A few days later she woke up in the middle of night and through the darkness she saw a shadowy figure of what she believed to be a man. The dark figure just stood in a corner looking in my mother's direction. It scared the crap out of her and she wasn't able to sleep all night. No one was there, but a few weeks later, a guy just up from Oaxaca started to follow her around. My dad threatened him, but one night when he was out in Sonoma and my mom was alone, he broke into the house. He didn't hurt her, he just stared at her while she slept. She started screaming and he ran away. They never saw him again, but after that, my mom listened to my *Mamita*. I have the power to predict things too, and I have very vivid dreams that come true. Last night I had a vision of a woman in red floating above my bed with snakes coming out of her eyes," she said as she finally stood up. "I have a very strong feeling I know who has the bad juju. I can feel the bad vibes coming out of someone's soul right in this very house. The danger is leaking out of their pores. Can you feel that?"

Mattie stared at the flexible young woman whose eyes were bulging out of her head. "What the hell are you even talking about, Belinda?"

IV

udrey was in her bedroom, the door locked as she had promised. She opened her computer and typed:

"I am stuck on an island with dead and breathing vixens and it's scaring the hell out of me. Jill is dead, murdered by someone here. I know it's one of us, and I'm positive the murders are not over. Three down, seven to go I suppose. Everyone suspects each other but I know who the killer is...

She sat for a while without moving, staring at a picture hanging in her room. It was a Gauguin for sure, a woman lying nude in bed while two other woman stood in the background and a raven on the windowsill. It wasn't the raven of Edgar Poe, but a bird of the devil who watches. The painting deeply disturbed her. Finally she began to type again, in all caps. "THE MURDERER'S NAME IS GEORGE AUSTIN!!!!

Her eyes closed and her head dropped to her chest. A noise downstairs woke her with a start. She looked at the computer screen. She read what she had written and deleted the last sentence. "Did I write that?" she whispered to herself. "I must be losing my mind."

CHAPTER FOURTEEN

October 12

I

The next morning the storm had picked back up again and the wind and waves battered the beach, sending palm fronds into the pool. Small white caps tossed around on the surface as open umbrellas flew across the deck.

Sandra woke up before dawn. She had trouble sleeping and a nightmare about being trapped in a sauna had her tossing and turning until she finally woke up. Damn that she could hear Belinda talk of hocus pocus from her room. She didn't believe in any type of magic. She was frustrated that it even bothered her. She realized that she should just say the hell with it and go downstairs and make some breakfast for the others. She craved something healthy and decided to make her trail mix. Sandra slipped on a Juicy Couture black warm-up suit, UGG slippers and grabbed her rosary beads, tucking them into her pocket before she quietly walked downstairs. The house was dark except for a small lamp in the Great Room that she had left on the night before, so she tread lightly. She paused at each of the deceased vixens rooms and made the sign of the cross.

The kitchen was cold, even though the rest of the house was warmed by the humidity, so she turned on the oven. She stepped into the pantry and found nuts and brown sugar and dried fruit. In the refrigerator, she noticed the fruit and vegetables were few, but there were 20 or so packages of lunch meat. She took one out and read the label.

"Devon," she read aloud. "It looks like baloney," she said, crinkling up her nose in disgust. She tossed it on the counter and began gathering the ingredients for the convent's Heavenly Granola. They sold it to local shops in San Francisco and Marin. The convent was famous for it, and even though she helped make it every week, it was a change from the everyday drudgery in the nunnery. Each morning, Sandra and the other nuns had to rise at four to pray, turning in at 11 at night to sleep on single beds with only a thin mattress. To help them support themselves, the nuns would bake granola and trail mix and sell it in three-pound bags at the local farmer's market. The granola and the trail mix were pretty much the same thing, so she decided to use what she had on hand and the vixens could eat it for breakfast and munch on it in the afternoon at wine time.

Pulling out the ingredients and spices brought back memories of not only her life as a nun, but before, when she convinced her father that he was making the right decision for his daughter. She knew he needed her at home after her mother died giving birth to her youngest sister, Mary-Elizabeth. Her father drank away his sadness and occasionally took it out on Sandra. He would slap her now and then if she sassed him, but other than that, he didn't pay any attention to her. He expected the house to be clean as well, as her siblings. It was her job as the eldest daughter. The convent, while boring and stifling, had saved her life.

She found a large, beautiful teak cutting board and went to work hacking the pecans and walnuts with a sharp Wusthof knife she had found on the counter. The sun was just beginning to rise and she could see a ribbon of orange and gold peeking through the grey, angry clouds. *Maybe today will be a better day*, she thought. Maybe today she would find a way to get off this God-forsaken island.

II

Cookie woke up to the smell of coffee and something sweet and nutty. She jumped out of bed with a smile and climbed into the large walk-in shower. She placed a shower cap over her thin hair and turned on the hot water. The scent of Kai body wash she used brought back fond memories of the two weeks she and Kurt spent in Maui and her mood improved even more. When she toweled off she found a pair of Vimmia Solstice Strength Pants and a Sweaty Betty Athlete Workout Tank, but the pants seemed to have shrunk and she couldn't quite pull them over her hips. She looked around and grabbed a loose beach cover-up she had bought on at Becky's Bikini's in Santa Barbara. She decided she could stop dressing for the vixens and be comfortable for a change. She sponged on some foundation and squinted in the mirror, looking for stray facial hairs. Satisfied, she ran her finger over a single line near her eye and did her best to frown. She would have to make an appointment as soon as she returned to the States for some fillers to abolish the nasty laugh lines. She vowed to stop smiling so much. Cookie added some bronzer, clear lip-gloss, and slipped her feet into her Nike flip-flops. Her stomach growled and she realized that she needed a little something to eat before she went to the exercise room. She planned on staying down there most of the day as a way to avoid the other vixens. Especially Tracy, who for some reason had a bug up her ass. She couldn't understand it. Even through all the major breakups of the group, Tracy had her back. She always assured her she was right and everyone else was wrong. She listened to her rant and rave about Audrey, who 10 years earlier had really started to get on her nerves. Audrey thought she was so smart. And damn if her ten-year age difference didn't piss her off as well. Cookie would make a deal with the devil if she could be 39 again like her former friend. Audrey wasn't beautiful, but she was pretty. She hadn't had any major work done yet, and she seemed to judge Cookie every time she had a facelift or an eye job or a neck peel. Good thing she didn't know about the work down below her tummy tuck or she'd never hear the end of it. As if being on TV Audrey wouldn't start to do the same damn procedures she mocked her for having done at her age. That Audrey could be so judgmental. She did have her good points though. When Cookie was recovering from her first boob job, Audrey had brought over cute little ice packs for her swollen breasts, and a vintage red halter top. She also went with her to bail her mom out of jail when she had a breakdown in Nordstrom's. That was so humiliating for Cookie. Veronica had tried to put $5000.00 worth of clothes on Cookie's credit card. When the salesperson called security, Veronica started screaming and tearing her clothes off. They called the cops and Veronica was brought in on a 5150—which Cookie found out was the cop code for crazy. Audrey had been sitting by the pool with her at Cookie's first house she owned with Kurt, a cute little four bedroom near the beach in San Diego. Cookie had been so freaked out that Audrey drove to the jail and took charge. When Veronica walked out, she hugged Audrey like a long-lost daughter and thanked her for 'springing her.' She ignored her actual daughter. Cookie shook the memory out of her head and walked out of her room. As she strode down the hall to the staircase, she quickly walked past the rooms that held the dead women, shivering a tiny bit as she passed Jill's room.

"You kind of deserved it," she whispered as she walked by Jill's door.

As she walked down the steps, the scent of something burning tickled her nose and she hustled faster toward the kitchen.

"Who the hell is crucifying the toast this early in the morning?" she said, turning the corner before she came to a stop. Sandra was on her stomach. A pool of blood surrounded her and a large butcher knife stuck out of her back. Cookie screamed so loud she thought she might burst a blood vessel. She quickly scurried away from the former nun. She swiveled her head and spied the vixen wine glasses on the bar. Her eyes flitted back and forth, counting. She came up with six glasses and she felt an anxiety attack coming.

"Goddammit, another dead vixen!" she yelled as the others came running in. "What is going on and why do you hate us so much?" she yelled at them all.

III

Mattie didn't have to pronounce Sandra dead, as everyone could see she was gone. Cookie sat shivering in the corner of the room, drinking a cup of coffee with brandy in it that Audrey had made for her. All the others kept an eye on her, watching her pour both the coffee and the brandy.

"I'm going to look for something to wrap her in," Jerdie announced. "Everyone else stay here. Watch each other. I feel safer going off on my own." The women nodded and watched Cookie, doing their best not to look at the dead woman on the floor.

"What was she doing up so early?" Belinda said.

Tracy walked to the oven and pulled out the burnt fruit and nuts.

"It looks like she was making her trail mix."

"Oh," Belinda said. "I liked her trail mix."

The women nodded and waited for Jerdie to return. When she did, carrying a new shower curtain still in the package, they breathed a sigh of relief.

"I found this in a storage room. I think if we wrap her in it, the blood won't get all over the place. We have to take her to her room."

"Do we take the knife out of her back?" Cookie said.

Belinda giggled. "She was literally stabbed in the back. Makes sense."

The vixens stared at her.

"Too soon," Tracy admonished, resisting a smile.

"Sorry."

Tracy, Jerdie and Audrey rolled Sandra in a shower curtain decorated with brightly painted flamingos, birds of paradise and palm trees.

"That must be for the maids' bathrooms," Cookie said. "It's *très* tacky."

Audrey looked up and locked eyes with her nemesis.

"Your empathy is, overwhelming as is your sympathy."

"Fuck you Audrey," Cookie said taking a drink of her coffee. "I'm in shock, so back the hell off."

Audrey shook her head in disgust. She leaned down to help the others lift the nun who was rolled up in the shower curtain like a fancy cannoli. They headed toward her bedroom.

"You all better come with us," Jerdie said.

Belinda stood up and followed the death march, but Cookie

remained seated.

"I'm fine here as long as you are all together," she said waving them away. "I will not let the terrorist win."

"It's your funeral," Belinda said, making eye contact with Tracy. "Sorry."

IV

The vixens placed Sandra face down on the bed, wrapped in the shower curtain and with the knife still in her back. They closed the window and turned the air conditioner up as cold as it would go.

"This place is really going to start smelling soon," Tracy said, as she locked the door and closed it behind her. "If a heat wave comes we're going to have to sleep outside in the maid's quarters."

"As if," Jerdie said. "My room is perfectly fine and we all have a/c and windows and French doors. I will not stoop to sleeping in the maid's room."

"Wow, first world problems much?" Audrey said.

Jerdie ignored the barb.

The women returned to the kitchen and found another nightmare. Cookie was lying on the floor face down, her cup shattered and coffee pooling near her head. Her long, spindly legs and arms were sprawled in a classic police chalk outline.

"Oh my God, I didn't spike her coffee," Audrey said loudly. "You all saw me!"

"Holy crap, this can't be," Mattie said, running to the vixen on the floor. The others quickly followed and Mattie gently turned Cookie over. The woman's eyes were closed and a beatific smile was on her unlined face. They looked at each other in alarm as Mattie felt for a pulse. She frowned.

"What the hell?" she yelled.

Cookie smiled, her bleached teeth grinning wide. She sat up quickly, nearly knocking into the vet.

"Gotcha!" she said, her eyes darting around quickly at the other women.

The vixens jumped back and began yell.

"What is wrong with you?"

"Are you crazy?"

"I will kill you myself if you do that again!"

Cookie smiled evilly.

"I needed some levity," she said. "And I wanted to see who cared about me. Who had, as Audrey so sweetly put it, 'empathy for poor, dead Cookie.'"

She stared at Tracy, who was standing the furthest away.

"I see my BFF hung back," she said. "So there's that. I mean, if you don't care if I'm dead I guess our friendship is as dead as Sandra."

Tracy stared back defiantly. "Sometimes the person you'd take a bullet for ends up being the person pulling the trigger," she said.

"What the hell does that mean?" Cookie asked stepping toward Tracy.

"You figure it out," Tracy said, turning away.

"Hey," Cookie yelled. "Hey, don't turn your back on me. We're not finished talking here."

Tracy turned. "Shut up, shut up, shut up!" she yelled, surprising them all. "I am sick of hearing you talk at me. I'm tired of your unsolicited advice and I am tired of hearing your annoying voice." She took a deep breath. "If we both somehow get out of here alive, I want you to know that you are dead to me." She turned and headed for the kitchen.

"Wait," Cookie said.

"Dead to me!"

V

Audrey stuck her head in the refrigerator and frowned. It was after one and they had skipped breakfast. They were getting low on fresh fruits and vegetables, although here was a plastic bag of leftover pineapple that had turned brown, and a mango that looked too mushy to eat. Other than that, it seemed as the women had scarfed down all of the healthy food. She sighed and walked to the pantry and opened it. There were the usual dry goods of beans and rice, cans of beans and corn and exotic spices along with the fancy salts and peppers. She glanced at the top of the cupboard and noticed a whole shelf devoted to one item, but she didn't have her reading glasses. She grabbed a step stool and climbed up to grab a can. She read the label and chuckled.

"What are you cackling about, did you find a new way to poison us?" Cookie asked, standing close behind Audrey. Cookie had changed into short jean shorts and a halter-top. If Audrey wasn't mistaken, there was a hint of a muffin-top squeezing out of the Lucky brand shorts. Cookie's hair was piled on top of her head and her temples sported tiny streaks of grey.

"No Cookie, it's an entire shelf of devon," she said showing her the can.

"What's that? Like Spam or something? I saw a bunch of it in the fridge too."

Audrey smiled. "I suppose, kind of, but really it's more like bologna. Devon sandwiches are to Australians what bologna is to Americans."

Cookie glanced at the stacked cans lined up neatly and smirked. "So what you're saying is, that this is all a bunch of baloney?"

"So it seems Cookie, so it seems."

VI

Audrey made two devon sandwiches as Cookie watched her every move. Two slices of French bread were slathered with a tomato sauce that she found next to the tins of meat. Audrey opened all of it with a can opener under Cookie's watchful eyes. She plopped each sandwich on a Limoges plate and slid one over to Cookie.

"You know what I think?" Audrey asked after she took a bite and chewed it slowly.

"Since you're about to tell me I won't try and guess," Cookie said, devouring her sandwich.

Audrey ignored her.

"I covered a mass murder in Charleston a few years ago. Five young sorority sisters were murdered in the middle of the night and no one heard a thing until the morning when a neighbor starting screaming when she noticed a body in the front yard. It was one of the sorority girls, who had been shot in the back. The cops had no idea what happened in the house. No screaming, no gunshots, nada. Anyway, there was only one girl left and she was a mess. Straight A student, member of the choir and a Sunday school teacher. She had slept through the whole thing. She was so sweet and innocent that even though they found her DNA all over the place, they acquitted her. And they never found any other suspects." She paused. "When you saw Sandra lying there, you freaked out and started to scream because that would be the natural reaction to finding the fourth body in two days lying on the floor in a pool of blood."

"So?"

"So, even when you pulled that stunt and we all thought you had been killed, one of us stood back calmly and quietly, as if she knew you couldn't be dead. It was as if she knew how the murders were going down and your little drama scene wasn't in the script."

Cookie sighed. "That's not proof that Tracy is the killer. It can be any of you."

Audrey raised her eyebrows.

"What?"

"Any of us?"

"Yes," Cookie said slowly. "I know it's not me."

"Well if that's how we're figuring this out, I doubt anyone here is going to admit they're the killer."

"But if you want to know the truth, I don't think you're the killer either."

"Really? Wow, that's a surprise coming from you."

"At first I thought it was you," Cookie said, standing up and walking around the concrete kitchen island to cut herself another slice of devon and putting it into her mouth. "Damn, this stuff is addicting. Anyway, I thought you being the killer was a little obvious."

"Because I'm on TV?"

Cookie rolled her eyes. "No, Jesus, get over yourself. I thought it was too obvious because you were the one who was so angry at me and mad at the others. You already killed the group."

Audrey thought about Cookie's theory.

"I guess I don't think you're the killer because, umm, well..."

Cookie stopped eating and stared daggers at Audrey.

"What, you don't think I'm smart enough to make all the plans and carry out all these murders?"

Audrey looked at her nails.

"I did it before and got away with it, so I'm pretty sure I'm smart enough to do it again," Cookie mumbled, but Audrey heard her plainly.

"Excuse me, what did you say?"

Cookie took the last piece of devon on the plate, swiped it through the last of the tomato sauce and stuffed it in her mouth.

"I didn't say a damn thing Audrey. Not a damn thing."

VII

Belinda finished her run and plopped down in a cushy outdoor chair facing the Shearwater Garden. She wiped her forehead with the towel she had been carrying and took a big swig of water from her Camel Bak backpack. She blew out her breath and her eyes focused on the flowers. Sandra's death had really freaked her out. Running six miles didn't seem to erase the picture in her mind: the former nun on the floor with a knife in her back. Man, that was a tough way to go. Actually, everyone had died gruesome deaths. Belinda shivered and thought of the poem. Fucking poem, predicting all of the deaths. And the next one, death by bee? Well, that wouldn't be her fate. She wasn't allergic to bees, but Jill was. But Jill hadn't been killed by a bee. That was strange, she thought. Maybe the killer had confused Jill with someone else and bashed her head in instead of unleashing a bee in her room. Whatever, she needed to figure a way to get off the island—or at least hide from the other women until someone came to rescue them. Unfortunately, the gorgeous mansion sat on a damn rock. Outside of the trees, bushes, and flowers that surrounded the property, there wasn't anything else on the island. The island was literally a rock, surrounded by water. If she wandered too far from the house, she would starve or die of thirst. That wouldn't work. Damn.

Belinda took another sip of water. It was warming up again, and it was humid. Her hair was starting to frizz and she knew she would have to straighten it with her flat iron at least two more times before she went to bed. Damn curls. And her skin was dry as well. She couldn't seem to put enough Fresh Lotus moisturizer on her face, or Nuxe oil on her body. You would think this damn resort or mansion or haunted house would at least have softer water. When she got home, she was going to give this place a negative Yelp review. That is, if she ever got home. *Carajo*, she was scared! Everyone was being murdered and she just couldn't figure out who the bitch was who wanted them dead. Audrey could be her first choice, but she didn't seem really like the type. She was always nice to Belinda and had her back when Jill or Cookie said nasty things to her face. Of course, Audrey could have been talking shit behind her back as far as she knew. And Cookie, there was a murdering *puta* if there ever was one, but why would she care? She thought her shit didn't stink and she didn't care if she didn't have any friends. She had her money, her big house and her husband, who she bossed around. She'd never had any other friends, so she was used to it. And the other vixens? Tracy was too nice, but was she angry inside after years of being in Cookie's shadow. How about Mattie? She could be the one. She was a little out there...really smart, but she said the weirdest things sometimes. Like she had the Tourette's or something. Jerdie was just plain stuck-up, but that didn't make her a killer. No, there had to be someone else on Vanishing Island. Belinda took a few more cleansing breaths and noticed something in the flowers. She moved her body closer to a group of pink lilies and laughed. It was a bee. A little, tiny bee looking for nectar in the lush petals.

"As if I'm afraid of a bumble bee," Belinda said, laughing and throwing her head back slightly. That's when she felt a tiny, familiar prick and her eyes widened, one last time.

CHAPTER FIFTEEN

———

Laverne—Dead
Justine—Dead
Jill —Dead
Sandra —Dead
Belinda— Dead

I

Jerdie walked into the kitchen and found Cookie, Audrey, Mattie and Tracy bustling around the kitchen.

"What are you guys doing?" she asked, feeling left out.

"We're taking an inventory of what we have left to eat," Mattie said, opening the pantry. Audrey and Cookie rustled through the refrigerator as Tracy took notes.

"I want to help," she said.

"Sure, come help me in here," Mattie replied." I can't see up on that top shelf, but whatever it is we have a lot of it."

Jerdie stood on her tiptoes, turned one of the cans around and read the label.

"Oh hell no!" She said, laughing. "I will not eat devon, especially in a can."

"What? Why not?" Mattie asked, grabbing a bag of rice.

"Because it's gross. It's like baloney and I will not eat baloney. I had enough of it when I was a kid. Fried baloney, baloney sandwiches, powdered eggs and baloney. Yuck. Absolutely not!"

Cookie raised her head. "Really? I thought it was pretty damn good."

Jerdie looked at the ex-beauty queen and was sure she could see a few extra pounds on her thighs. *Serves her right,* she thought.

"There's plenty here for all of us," Mattie said. "And lots of rice and beans."

Tracy looked at the meager amounts of fruits and vegetables that were sitting on the counter, then down at her list. She grimaced.

"It looks like we have plenty of booze, beans, bread and canned baloney and that's about it," she said. "Everything fattening."

"I don't think we have to worry about calories here," Mattie said. "Besides, we have to eat three meals a day to keep our strength up in case we have to run away or hide. We have to keep the booze intake down as well so no one can sneak up behind us and..."

"Smash our heads in?" Cookie asked.

"Poison our wine?" said Audrey.

"Smother us with a pretty pillow?" said Tracy.

"Stab us in the back?" smirked Jerdie. The other women winced at the last example. They turned and looked at the vixen wine glasses on the table.

"Fuck me!" Jerdie yelled as she looked around wildly. "There's only five glasses." She looked around quickly. "Where's Belinda?"

Everyone froze.

"She went for a run," Tracy said, looking at her watch. "About three hours ago."

The women raced through the house calling Belinda's name. After a few minutes they met up in the kitchen, panic etched on all of their faces.

"We need to look outside," Audrey said. "But let's stay together. This is terrifying and I for one am scared out of my mind."

Jerdie started to cry. "I want to go home to my nana," she said. "I don't want to die. I loved my sister but I didn't try hard enough to help her because I'm a selfish bitch."

Tracy put her arm around Jerdie. "It's OK, you did the best you could. She didn't want help so what could you do?"

"No, you don't get it, the voice was right about me. And about Birdie. I lied to you the other night. Right before I left, my nana called me and told me that Birdie overdosed in a hotel. I didn't have time to wire her money for the rehab that she wanted to check herself into or find her a place to detox. I told her to hole up in a nice hotel and detox. I mean, how hard could it be?"

"Really?" Cookie asked. "How many days can you go without a glass of vino?"

Tracy shot her friend a dirty look. "You couldn't have known," she said hugging Jerdie harder, but Jerdie pushed her away.

"I did know, I did!" She screamed. "But I was tired of her being an addict. I was tired of everyone blaming me for stealing her fiancé and marrying him."

"But that's exactly what you did," Cookie said under her breath.

"She was funnier than me, and smarter," Jerdie said, wiping her nose with her sleeve. "She was way more popular than I was in high school, and even college. When she started using, I saw it as my chance to be the best twin. When she asked for money for drugs, I always gave it to her. I pretended to believe her when she said she had her habit under control. When she started sleeping in the streets I would go look for her when my nana guilted me into it, but I didn't look very hard. When I finally paid for a high profile rehab in Los Angeles, she begged me to come and get her after only a week. She said she was being sexually abused but I didn't believe her. When she ran away from that place, I disowned her. A year later, she called me collect and told me about a nonprofit rehab for women. It wasn't expensive at all and she said she had gone to a meeting and was accepted into a six-month program, but she needed $800 and a place to detox. I laughed at her, told her she was a liar, and if she wanted to get clean, she could go get a room at the Motel 6 for a few days and detox. I called the hotel and gave them my credit card number, then called Uber to pick her up. Ten days later Nana called me and told me she was dead. My sister died in a Motel 6 and it's my fault. The voice was right," she cried. "I killed her!" She dropped onto a couch and sobbed. The other women were silent and let her cry it out.

Finally, Audrey cleared her throat. "OK. Well, shall we go outside and look for Belinda?"

The others nodded their heads and Jerdie sat up, wiped her eyes with the back of her hand and adjusted her plain black T-shirt over her black jeans.

"Yes, let's go look for her," she said, pulling herself together.

As they walked through the door Tracy held out her hand, but Jerdie brushed past her and walked faster to catch up with the others.

II

After searching for 20 minutes, they found Belinda sitting peacefully in the garden. The pink flowers were a delicate contrast to the sky, which was slowly turning gold and red as the sun began its descent. She looked like she was resting after an exhausting workout, her water pack at her feet. Mattie let out an audible sigh of relief.

"Hey *chica*, we were worried about you," Jerdie said as they approached the vixen. Then, as the women moved around to face her, they saw her blue lips and dead eyes staring off into nothing. A syringe was stuck in her forehead.

"Dead." Audrey whispered.

"Quell surprise," Cookie said.

Audrey and Cookie edged closer. Mattie stood back with Tracy and Jerdie.

Audrey pulled her sleeve down over her fingers and pulled the needle out of Belinda. Her head dropped to her chest and the two women jumped back. Cookie looked at the syringe.

"That's one of Belinda's Botox syringes," she said.

"She brought Botox to the island?" Tracy said. "Who does that?"

Cookie and Jerdie looked away.

"Do you think it was really Botox or some sort of poison?" Audrey said, addressing Mattie.

"How should I know?" Mattie said, her voice quivering. "She's dead. We can all see that she's dead. I don't have to take her pulse or listen for a heartbeat. We can all pronounce her dead. Right? Can we call agree on that?"

Jerdie stepped away. "Dude, chill out," she said. "You're freaking me out even more than I already am."

There was a buzzing from the pink lilies.

"Holy crap. A bee, a bumble bee, just like that fucking poem predicted," Cookie said. "Whoever planned all this and is bumping us off has a dark sense of humor." She looked at Tracy. "How about it Trace, you're a comedian, do you think this is all a big joke? Did you kill Belinda with bad Botox?"

"What?" Tracy said, her voice high and shrill, looking at the woman's accusing eyes. "No. No, I did not!"

CHAPTER SIXTEEN

Laverne—Dead
Justine—Dead
Jill—Dead
Sandra—Dead
Belinda—Dead

I

Audrey and Cookie carried Belinda to her bedroom and gently placed her on the bed. They pulled the sheet over her and turned up the air conditioner as the others had done previously. Audrey started to walk toward the door, but noticed Cookie picking up clothes from the floor.

"What are you doing?"

"I'm cleaning up. This is disgusting. It's bad enough that the newspapers are going to have a field day covering this story, but we don't need them thinking Belinda was a pig. I think that even if she was a major slob when she was alive, we should help her out now. We have our reputation to think about."

"Our reputation?"

Cookie stood up, a red lace thong in her hand. "You know what I mean. Belinda's reputation. Sheesh, give me a break, my nerves are frazzled and I need some damn wine."

Audrey stared at the tall beauty bending over, gathering clothes, folding them and putting them away.

"I'll get the wine and come back and help you."

Cookie looked at her, eyes wide. "You're leaving me here alone?"

"You want that wine or not?" she said, smiling. "Listen, lock the door and I'll knock three times. I'll bring an unopened bottle and two glasses and we can clean this up together. I won't be gone long. Deal?"

Cookie looked at the small body on the bed and back to Audrey. "Deal, but don't die. I might actually miss you."

II

Audrey walked downstairs to the sound of crying. Jerdie and Mattie were crying and Tracy was biting her nails. They were huddled together on the large couch under the ceiling fan. Jerdie had a blanket over her lap and Tracy was writing in a notebook. Audrey looked closer and saw that the women weren't as well put together as they had been when they arrived. Jerdie wasn't wearing any makeup, and her afro was flat on the sides and poofy in the middle. Mattie was wearing some hideous pajama bottoms with a white pink T-shirt with red sauce stains scattered about her top. Her hair was even worse: sticking out everywhere, reminding Audrey of a blooming onion. Tracy wasn't quite as bad, but she had dark circles under her eyes and her fingers were red from being bitten to the nub. *The wheels are definitely falling off*, she thought.

"You guys OK? Can I get you anything?" Audrey said.

Jerdie jerked her head up. "Do you hate us so much that you're killing us off?" she said. Audrey stepped back as the three women stared at her.

"No, I'm not the killer. I'm just as afraid as you are."

"I know, but you started this," Jerdie replied.

"I started what?"

"You killed the vixens back in the day by leaving us."

Audrey laughed. "Oh please. You all keep saying that, but it's not true. You continued with your little lunches for a year or two after I left. I didn't kill anything." She turned away and walked to the wine fridge. She opened it and saw two opened, half-finished bottles of La Crema Chardonnay. She had promised Cookie an unopened bottle and that's what she wanted as well.

"No, after you bolted, Cookie started having secret lunches with a chosen few," Tracy said. "She said there were too many of us, so she handpicked the people she would invite to her lunches and would only go to the big lunches every three months or so. She called us the cool kids."

"Really?" Audrey asked as she began searching for more wine.

"Yep, it was me and Jerdie and Belinda and Cookie. Everyone else was left out. And we had to keep it a secret. No selfies, no photos. It was uncomfortable and it didn't take long for Jill and Laverne to figure it out. I don't think Sandra cared, but that's when she stopped coming. I felt bad, but I knew if I said anything I would be left out, too."

"That was rather high school of her," Audrey said, finding a case of wine. She pulled a bottle out and frowned.

"Exactly, except she wasn't popular in high school at all," Mattie said, who had graduated with Cookie. "The other girls never liked her. She wasn't a cheerleader or in choir or band. Instead, she was in all those stupid pageants her mom forced her to enter. She always came in second or third place. Trust me, she didn't have many friends on the pageant circuit either."

"So you weren't invited to the secret lunches Mattie?"

The veterinarian laughed. "No, which was fine. I have a real job and saving lives of animals is a hell of a lot more interesting than drinking wine and talking shit about so-called friends. That's when I moved to Montana. I'd had it with California and people like Cookie."

"So see, I didn't kill the group, we all had a hand in it," she said, looking at the labels on the wine and shaking her head. This was not going to end well.

III

"N ooooo!" screamed Cookie as Audrey walked into the room. "I will not drink Two-Buck Chuck!"

"Calm down, Cookie, it's all we have left. We've been drinking the good stuff likes it was Diet Coke or something."

Cookie eyed the bottle as if it were arsenic.

"I need to get off this island," she said through gritted teeth, looking out in the dark night.

"Look, I brought ice and soda water too, so we can make it a spritzer. We can make it work. We have to make it work because vixens without wine might as well go jump in the ocean. Am I right?"

Cookie shrugged and sat down on the bed, accidentally sitting on Belinda's foot. She jumped up.

"Goddammit, why is this happening to me?"

"I don't know," Audrey said, wrestling with the cork in the bottle. She finally put it between her knees and pulled as hard as she could. "But someone clearly doesn't like the vixens."

"I don't like the vixens," Cookie said, taking a slug of her wine. "Jesus, I mean, we always had those damn lunches and air kissed everyone and talked about how perfect our lives were. All the perfection started to get nauseating. Audrey took a sip as Cookie watched her closely. She took a bigger sip and Cookie smiled.

"Just checking," she said, smiling.

"I get ya," Audrey said, laughing.

Cookie plopped onto the floor and looked down at her stomach. A tiny bit of flesh hung over her waistband.

"Well that's just great," she muttered as she undid the top button of her jeans. "That's better," she said, drinking the last of her wine and holding it out to Audrey for more. Cookie stared at Audrey. She noticed that her face was blotchy and she had a brown spot on her right cheek. Her hair was a little wild and she could see a few gray hairs on her temples. She realized she wasn't faring much better. She hadn't straightened her hair in days and her extensions were getting ratty. Her eyelash extension were drooping, making her eyes look hooded, which was not a good look. It was tough on a gal to keep up appearances when she was trying not to get murdered.

"Umm, Aud, what really happened to us? I mean, we managed to become friends again after Sean and I had our fling, but then we fell apart bad. What happened?"

Audrey poured soda water into the wine and shook her head. She handed the drink back to Cookie and locked eyes with her.

"Cookie, when you and Sean got together it hurt, but I knew he was ready to leave. I could tell. He didn't want to be married to me and

225

he hooked up with you to drive the last nail into the coffin."

Cookie stayed silent.

"I thought we were in it for the long run, you know? But then, he changed his mind about having kids and making more money than anyone in the office was his focus. When he did come home, he went to the gym or watched sports. You were his ticket out of our relationship. He really didn't love you, he just wanted to hurt me and you were going through midlife crisis at the time. No offense."

Cookie waved her off. "None taken. I knew what he was doing and he knew I was vulnerable, so we used each other, but we never slept together. Just emails and make-out sessions and secret dates. That was the thrill of it. It made Kurt sit up and take notice when he found out—oh, and thanks for that, by the way."

Audrey shrugged.

"Luckily Kurt forgave me and you are better off without Sean. He was kind of a dick."

"I know, but he was my dick, not yours."

"Back to my question though. We stopped speaking for like a year and then we ran into each other at the nail salon and ..."

"We went out for a drink and we talked it out and then we had to call Kurt to send a car!"

They both laughed and then looked away.

"I always liked your sense of humor," Audrey said carefully. "But after a few years it changed. You started to become unkind and sometimes cruel."

"I did not. You always seemed to know it all and it pissed me off royally."

"My intelligence makes you mad?"

"No…but you always had an answer or you corrected me when I was wrong."

"So, you would rather say ignorant things in public and look dumb? And we can't have an intelligent conversation?"

Cookie glared at her and then gulped down her wine.

"Fuck it," she said. "We're too different. We somehow managed to have a friendship for many years and then I think we both started to annoy each other, like an old married couple. Then we started to fight. It happens and it happened to us."

Audrey stared at the floor. "Yep, I guess that's what happened."

They were both silent for a moment and then Audrey spoke. "I heard your boys moved away," she said. "That must be tough on you. You were a good mom."

Cookie laughed bitterly. "Was I? Then why did they both feel they needed to move thousands of miles away from me? Kevin moved to Montreal to play baseball, although he was offered a contract with the Giants. I mean, he moved to another country!"

Audrey stayed silent.

"Kip and his friend—I mean boyfriend or whatever they are—

moved to Paris. I hate Paris. It's smelly and dark and French people live there." She shuddered. "Whatever, they don't come home ever and I refuse to be the one to cave in and go to them."

Audrey sat down on the floor next to Cookie. "I didn't know. Sorry."

Cookie wiped away a tear. "Shit, I've been so damn depressed for like, two years. Kurt works all the time and I wander the house by myself. I don't have any friends and my kids are gone. Some days it's all I can do to get out of bed."

She started to cry in earnest. Audrey wrapped her arms around her former friend and let her sob.

CHAPTER SEVENTEEN

October 13

I

The mood in the house was as dark as the sky. The sun hadn't yet made its morning appearance and the fog was like a thick blanket wrapped around the island. Mattie was at the stove cooking breakfast when Tracy walked in to get coffee. She looked at the empty pot and then at Mattie.

"You couldn't make coffee?" she asked sullenly.

"I could, but I didn't," Mattie replied. "Besides, there's only decaf. We ran out of the good stuff."

Tracy's eyes went wide. "Are you shitting me?"

Mattie shook her head and continued to cook.

"Do we have any caffeinated tea?"

"I didn't see any."

Tracy walked into the pantry and began searching.

"What's cooking?" she heard Jerdie say.

"Devon and eggs."

"Ewww, gross. Do we have anything else?"

"You can have toast and I found some of that vegemite."

"Absolutely not," Jerdie said. "I'll have dry toast and coffee I guess."

Mattie said loudly. "No coffee except decaf."

"No coffee, no caffeine anywhere," yelled Tracy from the pantry.

"Well, hell." Jerdie said.

"Yep," Mattie said.

Cooke entered the kitchen with Audrey following behind.

"Ladies," Audrey said, nodding her head. She walked to the coffee pot and stared.

"We're out of coffee," the three women said. Cookie looked up in horror. Audrey frowned and went to the refrigerator to look inside. "We have water, apple juice and milk," she said.

"That's great if we were toddlers," Cookie said. "Do we have some of that crap wine?"

Audrey pulled out a bottle and set it on the table. "We have a ton of this crap wine."

Cookie reached for a juice glass and an opener and poured a half of a glass of chardonnay. "Anyone care to join me?"

The women looked at her and then grabbed their own glasses.

"Why the hell not?" Tracy said.

II

C ookie ate her plate of eggs and devon with gusto as the other women picked at their breakfasts.

"Anyone have any bright ideas?" Audrey asked.

"About what?" Mattie mumbled.

"About getting off the island or protecting ourselves. You know— staying alive?"

The women were silent.

"Fine, I have an idea and it's related to trust."

"You want us to trust each other?" Jerdie, asked, her eyes darting around the table.

"I think we have to figure out how to depend on each other so we have a chance at staying alive," Audrey said.

"What do you have in mind?" Tracy asked.

"I think we need to search everyone's room to see what type of weapons or drugs that we're hiding so that we can all be positive that none of us is the killer. If we have dangerous items in our suitcases or rooms, we have to throw them in the ocean. And we should do it right now so we can't stash anything away." She looked at the vixens. "What do you think?"

"Sure."

"Fine."

"I don't care."

"And one more thing," Audrey said. "We need to do it naked."

Cookie spit out her wine and laughed.

"What the hell for?"

"Because we could hide something in our clothes or in our bras," Jerdie said, smiling.

"I'm not wearing a bra," Cookie said.

The others laughed. Mattie stood up, went to the pantry, and came back with a case of wine. "Someone get the ice and an opener. We can start in my room. This is getting very weird. I think we are going to need to turn this into a party, or it might get very ugly."

III

The vixens gathered in Mattie's room first, which was littered with dirty coffee cups and wine glasses. Empty wine bottles were also scattered all about the room.

"Whoa, that's where all the good wine went," Cookie said.

Mattie closed her eyes and whispered, "Sorry."

"It doesn't' matter," Audrey said. "I'm getting used to the cheap stuff. Anyway, we need to know what type of drugs you brought with you or anything else that can harm us. Are you cool with us going through your things?"

"Sure," Mattie said.

"Wait, "Jerdie said. "Take off your clothes."

Mattie laughed and stood up. She pulled off her Seattle Seahawks sweatshirt and wiggled out of her jeans.

"Undies too," Audrey said.

"Why?"

"Because I don't want to search your coochie. Come on, just do it. We all agreed."

"Fine."

She did as she was instructed and stood naked in the middle of her room, looking into the distance while the women searched her suitcases, under the bed, closets, dressers and under the rugs. Mattie poured herself a glass of wine and stood with her back against the wall.

"I have some meds in the bathroom," she yelled at the search party. "And a little pink thing of pepper spray under my pillow."

The women searched through the room as if they were at a closeout sale at Nordstrom's and met back at the bed with a small cache of items. Mattie walked back over and looked at the goodies.

Three prescriptions in other people's names were prominent.

"It's only Adderall," Cookie said. "Big deal. You can't poison people with ADD medicine."

"How do you know?" Audrey asked.

"Because I take it all the time."

"You have ADD?"

"No, it keeps her skinny," Tracy said.

"Was she talking to you?"

"No, but I answered for you."

Cookie just stared at her friend.

"So, Xanax and Klonopin, is that it?"

"And the pepper spray," Jerdie said, reaching under the pillow. "Is that it? No knives, guns or poison?"

Mattie shook her head and stood tall.

"It's not me, so it's obviously one of you," she said. "Let's move it," she said walking out of the room. The women followed.

IV

Audrey sat on a vanity stool and watched the women paw through her things. She slugged down her wine and reached for the bottle. She knew she didn't have anything in her room that would be cause for concern. Some vitamins that were clearly marked and nothing else. They could search all day and they wouldn't find anything.

"I'll take some more wine," Mattie said.

"Me too,"

"I'll take some."

"Me too," Cookie yelled from the bathroom. "Whoop, treasure," she said laughing as she came out waving a large, hot pink vibrator. "OMG, it's an electric dick," she said.

"Oh grow up," Audrey said, walking over and grabbing it. "This is very expensive, don't mess with it."

"Really, who the hell needs a dildo?" asked Cookie.

All the other vixens raised their hands.

"Seriously?"

"Of course. Are you going to try and tell us you don't have one?"

"I have a husband with very strong sexual desires."

"So?" Jerdie said. "How about in between? Like when you masturbate."

Cookie put her hands over her ears and squeaked. "I don't masturbate," she said.

The other women laughed.

"Of course you do, you big liar," Tracy said.

"I don't, I really don't," Cookie said.

"No wonder you're so mean," Mattie mumbled.

"What was that?"

"Nothing," Mattie said drinking more wine. "Not a thing, but I tell you, you've been missing out."

"No I haven't," Cookie said. "I have sex every morning with my husband."

"Morning sex?" Audrey asked. "That doesn't count for much."

"Wham bam thank you ma'am," sang Jerdie.

"No, wait, sometimes at night too. Oh who cares, you're all jealous because I have a hot sex life."

"If you say so," Audrey said. "But if we make it out of here I know what I'm buying you for your 60th birthday."

Cookies face went white. "Don't say that number," she said. "Never say that number to me again."

The other women looked at her serious face and broke out laughing again.

V

J erdie stripped quickly and the other women tried not to look at her perfect body, although she caught Cookie staring at her ass one too many times. She walked with her head held high and stripped her bed, pulled open her drawers and offered her suitcases to the search party. Nothing was found.

"Happy now?" she asked.

VI

By the time they arrived at Cookie's room they were drunk. Cookie's room was perfect. Her bed was made and all of her clothes were hung up according to color. Her shoes were lined up and her jewelry was hanging from a little black dress jewelry organizer.

"My mom liked a clean house, what can I say?" Cookie said. She lifted her glass to the ceiling. "May you be ironing sheets in hell, Mother Dearest," Cookie shouted.

"Settle the hell down and save that for your therapist," Jerdie said. "But this is impressive. Hey, did you clean your bathroom floor?"

Cookie ignored her, sat on the floor and stretched her long legs. She touched her toes.

"I am still bendy," she giggled.

"Especially for an old broad," Tracy said.

The room was silent and then Cookie laughed. "Screw you Tracy."

Tracy hopped up on the bathroom vanity and took center stage.

"That reminds me," she said. "There's these two old gals who had been friends since their 20's. Now in their 80's, they still got together to play cards a couple of times a week. One day they were playing gin rummy and one of them said, "You know, we've been friends for many years and please, don't be mad at me, but for the life of me, I can't remember your name. Please tell me what it is."

Her friend glared at her. She continued to glare and stare at her for at least three minutes. Finally, she said, "How soon do you need to know?"

The vixens hooted in laughter.

VII

N othing dangerous or evil had been found, and the drunk and naked vixens sprawled out in Cookies room as the sun threw off colors of orange, fuchsia and gold with ribbons of silver behind them.

"To quote Oprah, I know one thing for sure. There are no weapons of mass destruction in the possession of any of us five vixens," Cookie slurred.

"I think that was Bush. Or Cheney."

"Shut up Audrey," Jerdie said.

"We need to put the drugs and other shit in a safe place."

"Really? You think my Swiss army knife is a weapon?" Tracy asked.

"Might be," Mattie said.

"Wait, I thought we were going to throw it all in the ocean," Tracy said.

"Two things about that," Mattie said. "It can float back in and it's polluting the ocean."

"Seriously?" Cookie asked.

"But we might die, Mattie. Who cares about polluting the ocean?"

"I do. Even if we don't make it off this hellhole, other generations will have to live on this planet. We need to be responsible, even in this terrible time."

Jerdie groaned and rolled her eyes.

"Hey, there's a safe in here," Cookie said, standing up quickly. She almost tumbled and would have if Tracy hadn't grabbed her arm.

"I saw it. Hang on."

"I thought there wasn't a safe and that's why we threw my gun in the ocean."

"I know," Cookie replied. "I swear, I never noticed it until last night. Very weird. I think I'm losing it. A safe doesn't just appear."

Cookie walked precariously toward the open French windows and stopped a few steps before a large chair and knelt down.

"Look," she said. "And it has two keys and two locks. Oops," she said and she fell onto the floor. "That's gonna leave a mark," she giggled.

Audrey stood up and walked toward Cookie. The others followed and they all stared stupidly at the safe.

"Two locks?" Audrey asked, her eyebrows rising.

"Two keys," Mattie confirmed.

Jerdie went back to the bed and scooped up the various drugs, multiple syringes of Botox, two pepper sprays along with the little knife. She stuffed the items into the safe and closed the heavy door. She took the keys Cookie held and locked both locks. She then turned and gave one key to Mattie and one to Tracy.

"You two are the, ummm, strongest physically so you should both take the keys. If any of us wanted to beat you up for the key, I think you could take us. By the looks of the safe, it would be nearly impossible for any of us to break into the damn thing. Does everyone agree with this decision?"

The others nodded their heads.

"Good. Now who do I have to blow to get a drink on this damn island?"

VIII

Mattie raised her head from the bed and tried to remember where she was. She moved her hand, felt a foot, and sat up in alarm. It quickly dawned on her that she was on Vanishing Island and that her friends were with her. Or, rather, her former friends. There was once a bond—it may have run its course, but it was there once. A nostalgic sadness swept over her as she remembered the deaths of Sandra and Belinda and the others. She looked at the remaining vixens, asleep and naked on the large bed in Cookie's room. She stood up slowly. The other women started to stir and a few reached for blankets as she headed for the bathroom. As she closed the door, she heard Cookie say, "Oh my God, I can feel my liver." Mattie smiled as she sat down on the toilet and listened to the conversation as she peed.

"Why are we still naked?" Jerdie said.

"Where are my damn panties?" Cookie said. "And by the way, you guys are going to have to help me clean up this freaking mess. You're all pigs."

"God I hate that wine," muttered Tracy, kicking a bottle with her toe out of the way. "Someone must really hate me."

"Just you?" asked Jerdie. "I'm pretty sure we're all equally hated."

"It's not a contest," Cookie said as she threw on her robe and picked up an empty bottle. "I for one would like to know how we got so stinking drunk. I mean, other than drinking two bottles each of this cheap-ass wine and only eating breakfast."

"First you take a drink, then the drink takes a drink, then the drink takes you, "Audrey said.

"What the hell are you talking about?" Jerdie asked.

"It's a quote. F. Scott Fitzgerald."

"Of course it is," Jerdie said.

"Oh shut up with the quotes. Can't you just be normal and say you have a hangover like the rest of us?" Cookie said. "You see, that's what pisses us off. Quoting shit and acting like you're smarter than we are."

Mattie walked out of the bathroom. "She is smarter than the rest of us," she said. "In fact, I think she's so damn smart that she's the killer."

The others looked at Audrey, who shrugged her shoulders. "I can't prove I'm not," she said. "Unless I die. And I don't plan on dying, so…"

"So you admit it?" Mattie said.

"No, I don't admit it," Audrey said, ripping the sheet off the bed and wrapping it around her like a Greek goddess. "Just because I'm irritating, doesn't mean I'm capable of killing vixens. I'm just as scared as you are and I am going to do everything in my power not to die."

"Oh, for hell's sake, she's not the killer," Cookie said not looking at Audrey. "She's just annoying. I think it's someone else, and it's one of us in this room." She looked at the other women and sat down on the edge of the bed. "If I had to choose, I would say the killer is…"

The others looked expectantly at her.

"Tracy!"

Tracy screamed, "It's not me and you know it! It's not me, it's you!"

"It's not me you crazy bitch. You're just jealous of me. You always have been jealous. Because I was a beauty queen and all the boys liked me in school, I married a rich man, and I'm happy. And oh, I'm skinnier than you and everyone in this room!"

"You killed Heather," Tracy said. "You did, I know you did!"

"Well you killed, Kenny. You snitched on him."

"I hope you die," Tracy screeched and ran out of the room.

CHAPTER EIGHTEEN

I

Tracy burrowed deeper under her quilt. It was probably less than 60 degrees outside and the fog was still enveloping the island, but she was too lazy to get up and turn up her thermostat. The quilt felt comforting as she reread her favorite book, *Shopgirl* by Steven Martin. She loved the character of Mirabelle, and her sad little life. *""I guess I have to choose whether to be miserable now, or miserable later,"* Mirabelle says in the book.

"I love that line," Tracy sighed. She'd read the novella at least three times and planned on finishing it again as a distraction from the hellish nightmare that she found herself in, with seemingly no way out. God, she was sick of these women. If they were all going to die, she wished the killer would just get it over with, hopefully taking Cookie next. As she turned the page, she heard a loud boom, and her table lamp went dark. She sat up quickly and clumsily searched for the flashlight in the bedside table. She clicked it on as her heart pounded.

"What the hell?" She said. She moved her flashlight back and forth around the room and saw nothing. She realized she was trembling, and not from the cold. She slowly stood up and tried to think what she should do. There wasn't any noise from the other women so she assumed they were asleep. She hoped they were asleep anyway. She threw the light on her bed, found her robe and covered herself. She usually slept in the nude, but in the last few days, she had taken to sleeping in her bra and underwear in case she had to make a run for it. She stepped into her flip-flops, walked toward the French doors, and looked down at the pool area. All the lights were off and it was pitch black, the fog making it even harder to see anything.

"OK, we probably blew a fuse or a transformer or something electrical," she assured herself. "We're on an island and I'm sure this kind of stuff happens all the time. Or at least I hope it does and this isn't a scene out of *Friday the 13th*. Oh God, oh God, oh God. OK, get a grip." She took a breath, turned around, and shone the light around the room. She took a deeper breath and started to walk to the bedroom door.

"All work and no play makes Jack a dull boy," she said with a nervous laugh as she put her hand on the doorknob.

"I'm just gonna bash your brains in, I'm gonna bash em' right the fuck in." She turned the knob and slowly opened it.

"Come out, come out, wherever you are." She shone her flashlight quickly down the hallway.

"Redrum, redrum," she said as she willed her heart to stay in her chest.

She made her way to the staircase and held the banister with one hand, and her flashlight in the other shaking hand.

"Heeeeeeeeere's Johnny!"She put her foot on the last step and tried the light switch a few times.

"Worth a try," she muttered and walked to the dining room. The French doors were wide open, which made Tracy shiver. She took another step into the room and felt her whole body start to sweat. She felt a familiar dread deep in the pit of her stomach as she slowly aimed the flashlight at the dining table. Tracy closed her eyes for a second and then opened them.

Another vixen glass had disappeared.

"Oh no, please no," she said, frantically looking around the room. She took a step toward the glasses and then changed her mind and made a quick turn.

"I am out of here," she said as she turned back to the staircase, took a step and tripped. As she fell, she realized what was happening and screamed, losing the flashlight and landing on what she knew to be a body of a dead vixen, quickly thanking God that she wasn't the one on floor of the great room. This time.

CHAPTER NINETEEN

I

It was the moaning that woke Cookie. She rolled over on her side and put a pillow over her head, knowing that whatever or whomever it was, it couldn't be good. She counted to 10 and finally gave up, rising slowly from her bed. She pulled her underwear out of her butt, walked to the bathroom, sat down on the toilet and looked down at her toes as she peed. She noticed that the polish on her toenails was chipped, and her right baby toenail was ragged from when she had stubbed it out by the pool. She stared at her feet for another moment and then realized that she didn't give a damn. She stood up, walked to the mirror, and squinted at a red dot on her face.

"A pimple," she said to her reflection. "Seriously? At my age?" She stared harder at it and felt it with her fingertip, which she noticed had dirt under the nail. "Jesus-God, I am a mess," she said shaking her head. She picked up a brush and tried to run it through her hair, but her extensions were tangled. She felt the back of her head and wasn't surprised to find her bald spot. "Icing on the cake," she said as she tossed the brush and walked into her room. She looked for her robe, the one that said 'Vixen Cookie,' on the breast pocket, and tied the sash. She ignored a grease stain and something yellow on the robe that she didn't recognize, and walked out her bedroom door.

As Cookie passed Jerdie's door, she banged on it and yelled, "Wake up, there's drama in the house!" For good measure, she knocked on Mattie's and Audrey's doors, but Tracy's was already open and she frowned.

As she began to descend the stairs, the moaning grew louder and she realized that it was Tracy, so she took the stairs two at a time. As she entered the Great Room, her eyes immediately darted to the infamous wine glasses on the bar. One was missing.

"That's not good," she said.

Her eyes zeroed in on Tracy, who was on the floor, rocking back and forth, sobbing and moaning, holding the lifeless hand of Audrey. Audrey's head was tilted sideways, her eyes closed and an angry red hole in her forehead, a small amount of blood dripping out.

Cookie felt her throat tighten and her eyes began to tear up at the sight of her two best friends crumbled and broken on the floor.

"We're all going to die Cookie, all of us," Tracy sobbed.

Cookie knelt down and wrapped her arms around Tracy, hugging her close.

"Shhh," she said. "We're going to make it out of here," she whispered. "I can feel it. We're the tough ones."

Cookie sat back and wiped a tear from Tracy's face, then turned to Audrey and winced. She put her hand on her former friend's forehead and a smoothed away her bloody hair.

"I think I'm really going to miss you, Aud," she said. "For reals."

II

The four remaining vixens stood in the kitchen picking at a plate of cold devon and sipping wine as the sun slowly peeked through the mist. They ate without tasting, and hardly touched their wine.

"I'll never eat devon again," Mattie said.

"Never say never," Jerdie said, chewing the meat and grimacing. "I seriously thought Audrey was the killer. We're running out of vixens to accuse. I mean, as soon as I suspect someone, they freaking die. I might go crazy before someone kills me."

"I don't want to carry another vixen to her room," Tracy said, tears rolling down her cheeks. "I can't do this anymore. Audrey has to be the last one. At least she wasn't too heavy."

"No kidding, and now that the power is off the smell is going to be rank. I mean, six dead bodies," Cookie said. "It's going to get ripe in here. I put a rolled up towel in front of Audrey's door to keep the smell in her room, so I think we should do that for the rest of them. I don't want to have to sleep outside because it smells like a morgue in here."

"Empathetic as usual," Mattie said. Cookie rolled her eyes.

"Who brought the gun?" Jerdie asked. "I tossed mine, so one of you has one and hid it from us. This means whoever has the gun is the killer."

"We looked in everyone's room," Mattie said.

"But someone could have hidden it outside. That's what I would do, I mean, if I had a gun and I was a serial killer," Jerdie said.

They stared at each other.

"Four of us left and we're all suspects," Cookie said.

"I think I know who it is," Jerdie said.

"I have my suspicions," Mattie replied.

"I don't know what to think," Tracy said wiping her face. "But I want to be alone. I can't look at any of you anymore knowing you could be a cold-blooded killer." She grabbed some devon, wrapped it in a napkin, walked to the case of wine, and drew out a bottle. "I'm going to my room."

"So am I."

"Me too."

"You're not leaving me down here alone," Cookie said.

The vixens each grabbed a bottle of wine and some devon and together walked slowly up the staircase. When they arrived at the top, they all jogged to their rooms. The sounds of door locks clicking and moving furniture filled the hallway.

Four frightened vixens were barricaded in their rooms.

III

J erdie finished pushing a table up against the door and dropped on her bed in exhaustion. She sat back up and walked to the mirror.

"Damn, I look like crap," she said, touching the bags under her eyes. She stared for a minute longer and touched her face. "Oh my God, my face is ashy, just like nana's!" She could almost hear her nana now. *"Damn, Jerdie skin be ashy...you need some cocoa butter to moisten up."* She shuddered and sat on the side of her bed. Her skin quite honestly was the least of her worries. Someone was going to try to kill her eventually. Probably sooner than later, since there were only four vixens still alive. Still, ashy skin was bad, so she pulled opened the drawer to her bedside table, but instead of L' Occitane Shea Butter, she stared down at her pink revolver.

IV

Cookie was on her bed on her back, staring at the ceiling. She noticed a big black hook over in the corner. She couldn't remember seeing it before. Was there a plant hanging from it earlier? How did she not notice it? Was her room now haunted or something? Damn, she was losing it. She put up a brave front downstairs, but she was scared out of her mind. She had finished off her Xanax after Belinda had been killed, and the booze was the only thing holding her together. She looked at the hook again, her breathing started to hasten, and she sat up in alarm.

"Hold it together, Cookie, you've got this. No one can come through that door unless you open it. I'm safe now. I can stay here for days. I don't need food, hell, I can stand to lose a few pounds anyway. I've grown fat. I must be a size four, for God's sake. But the wine, what will I do without wine?" She started to feel dizzy. "Stop, just stop," she said. "I'll figure out a plan and Tracy and I will find the killer. Unless it's Tracy. Shit, what if it's Tracy?" Her breathing continued to hasten. She stood up and walked to the bathroom, turned on the faucet and splashed cold water on her face. Once and then twice. Her breathing slowed a little and she ran her wet hands through her hair and reached for a towel. As she did, she noticed something was strange about the bathroom. The floor was wet, as if someone had

259

taken a shower and walked on the tile without drying. She took a small step toward the large tub toward and froze. The tub was full of water. She took another step closer and looked down. She grabbed the towel rack to keep herself from falling, and prayed she wouldn't pass out. Maybe she was hallucinating. She opened her eyes and it was still there. A sparkling silver pageant crown lay at the bottom of the filled bathtub. Cookie closed her eyes and slid down the wall, hyperventilating and sobbing quietly on the bathroom floor.

V

Mattie woke up to singing birds, relieved that she had made it through the night. She had tossed and turned until late, trying to get her head around the deaths and the fear and the why. Why were these former friends being murdered? Who was so hateful and sick that they wanted them dead, and why in the hell couldn't they figure out who the killer was and where they were hiding?

She was scared, but she was also mad. Mattie considered herself an intelligent woman. She had gone to college for more than eight years and graduated at the top of her class at Washington State. She was revered by her colleagues and her patient's owners. She was also a member of MENSA, so why couldn't she figure out this puzzle? But then again, no one had any ideas, even though it was almost guaranteed that one of the other three vixens was a serial killer. What they needed to do was get off the island as fast as they could. Even if they had to swim. Well, maybe not swim, considering there were sharks in the damn ocean. Even Mattie, who had been a competitive swimmer in high school and college, couldn't swim the 25 miles back to Sydney. She did, however, have an idea. She jumped out of bed, threw on some dirty shorts and a wrinkled white T-shirt she found on the floor, and walked out of her room.

"Yo, ho's, wake up, we're getting out of here today!" she yelled, walking down the hall. "Get up and meet me downstairs if you're not dead because I have a plan."

VI

Mattie walked into the great room with confidence in her idea. She tried not to look at the remaining glasses, but her eyes quickly counted them. Four, just like there were last night. Well, that was reassuring. No murders in the last five hours. The murderer must be tired.

She walked into the kitchen and opened the refrigerator. She stepped back as the smell hit her. Not everything was spoiled, but the last of the milk and the lettuce were getting ripe. She closed the door and Cookie walked in.

"What's up?" She mumbled. "No one died last night, according to those fucking glasses."

"I have an idea, but I need something to eat before I tell you my idea."

"Fine, whatever you say." Cookie opened the refrigerator. "Ugh. Gross," she said, turning away.

Jerdie and Tracy walked into the kitchen together.

"Yay, we all made it through the night," Jerdie said sarcastically.

263

"Woo hoo," said Tracy quietly.

Cookie walked to the case of wine and stared down at it.

"Jesus, I'm so depressed I don't even want any wine," she said, walking to the sink and filling a wine glass with water.

The other vixens grabbed glasses and filled them with water as well. Mattie pulled herself up on the kitchen counter and the other women waited for her to speak.

"As you know, we need to get the hell out of here. Since we can't swim, and other than this house, there's nowhere to hide on the island, we need to try and get someone to rescue us."

"And, how will we do that?" Tracy asked.

"Mirrors." Mattie said, pleased with herself.

"Are we going to put on makeup or something?" Cookie sneered.

"No, she's talking about Morse code and using mirrors," Jerdie said. "But do any of us know Morse code?"

They looked at each other and no one responded.

"No, but that's fine, we have so many mirrors that if we position them right a plane or a boat is bound to see it," Mattie said. "And the fog lifted. That's got to be a good sign

"I don't have anything else to do," Tracy said, shrugging her shoulders.

"That's the spirit," Mattie said. "Let's get cracking. Grab any and all mirrors you can drag outside and I'll meet you on the beach by the pool-house. This is going to work, I can feel it. I'll bet by this time tomorrow we'll be on our way home."

"If you say so," Cookie said, shuffling up to her room to tear a mirror off her wall.

VII

Jerdie walked to a large mirror on the wall decorated in gold with a garish pineapple theme, wondering why she hadn't noticed it before. "Ugh, that is tacky," she said aloud. "My nana wouldn't even have it in her house, and nana loves tacky." She stopped for a moment and thought about her nana, whom she truly loved. Her nana was really the only person who really loved her. And her sister Birdie. But Birdie was gone. Jerdie might die as well, and that would break Nana's heart. Jerdie knew it would, in fact, kill her grandmother. Losing two grandchildren—whom she had raised as her own after losing her own daughter, a nurse killed in battle in Vietnam—would be too much for the old woman. Jerdie wiped the tears from her face and took a deep breath. She stared at her reflection in the mirror. She looked horrible. She took another deep breath and screamed as loud as she could, as she yanked the mirror from the wall.

VIII

Tracy heard Jerdie scream and closed her eyes. It sounded more like a rebel call than a scream of terror, but Tracy didn't want to know. Jerdie was either alive or she wasn't. She couldn't do a damn thing about it either way. The only thing she wanted to do was stay alive, but the odds of that happening didn't look good. "And then there were four," she whispered. "Then three, and two and one. And then," Tracy whispered, picking up a mirror that sat on the mantel above the fireplace. "And then there were none." She shivered and walked out of her room.

CHAPTER TWENTY

Laverne—Dead
Justine—Dead
Jill—Dead
Sandra—Dead
Belinda—Dead
Audrey—Dead

I

After two hours of yanking and pulling and dragging mirrors onto the beach, but far enough up near the patio so the tide wouldn't wash them away, the women began standing mirrors up in the sand. They propped the big ones up with patio chairs and the small ones with rocks. They placed the mirrors in every direction, including straight up into the sky. There were only a few hours left before the sun would be starting to set, but Mattie, now full of hope, had encouraged them to gather wood to build a fire.

"If the mirrors don't catch their attention, a big fire might," she said. "And we'll do this every day until they come for us. Think of it, vixens. We'll be rescued and we can sell our stories to Steven Spielberg. I mean, if this isn't the perfect script for slightly older actresses like Nicole Kidman and Cate Blanchet, I don't know what is," she said.

"I think she's lost her mind," Cookie whispered to Tracy.

"Halle Berry can play me," Jerdie said. "She's been through a lot being a black woman in the movie industry, with the pain of her love life and all of her husbands. I think we would probably become best friends."

"Are you hearing this shit, Tracy?" Cookie muttered as she tossed a wooden table onto the woodpile.

"I think Amy Schumer could play me," Tracy said. "We're both blond and comedians."

"And you're like 25 years older than she is," Cookie said, laughing aloud at the thought.

Tracy turned her back on her friend. "Really, I think she would get me."

"I can see that," Jerdie said, nodding and moving a mirror with her foot.

"And you know who I think would be a great Cookie?" asked Jerdie. The others waited and Cookie rolled her eyes.

"Goldie Hawn," Jerdie said with a crooked smile.

"Are you out of your mind?" Cookie yelled. The other women started laughing. "She's like, 75 or something. I am not going to have an actress 20 years older play me, you can count on that. No way would Kurt let that go down."

"Seriously though, I think you might have had more plastic surgery than Goldie, so you can bond over that on the set," Tracy said through her laughter.

Cookie started to say something, and then she began to laugh.

"Good Lord, what the hell am I saying? If I get off this fucking island and Goldie Hawn wants to play me in a movie about our lives, then hell yes, bring it on!"

The other women cheered. Mattie threw a match on the fire and they cheered some more.

"I think we may very well go crazy before we get rescued, but at least we're in this together," Tracy said, smiling at Cookie. "At least we haven't killed each other."

II

Four vixens sat around the bonfire and staring up at the stars. They had brought wine out to the beach, but no one poured any.

"I'm going to miss good old Laverne," Cookie said.

"Are you kidding me?" Mattie said. "You said so many horrible things about her and you were always trying to ditch her, so why in the hell would you say that?"

"I don't actually know," Cookie said, twisting her hair with her fingers. "But she was like an annoying older sister, you know? She had some good qualities. I mean, she always brought appetizers to a party. Although honestly, her shrimp was usually a little old and bordering on spoiled, so maybe that's not it."

Jerdie laughed.

"Maybe because she adored you and Kurt. She thought you guys were like socialites or something. For some damn reason she worshipped the ground you walked on."

"That's it!" Cookie said. "That's what I miss."

271

The vixens groaned.

"I'm sure you'll find someone else to follow you around once we get off this island," Tracy said. "But it won't be me. We're going to have to take a break, Cookie. I'm going to need some time to figure out why I hang out with you when you're such a bitch. I need to find out why I put up with it and what the hell my problem is that I need a friend who verbally abuses me."

"Whatever, Tracy. I don't care. You know where to find me when you want to come back. Anyway, I plan to move to Palm Springs when we get back. It's as far enough away from the ocean as I can get and still be in civilization."

"That's if we get back," Jerdie said.

Tracy poked the fire with a piece of driftwood and began to sing.

*"Maybe we're standing on the threshold
With our eyes open wide..."*

"Shoot, I can't remember the rest of the words," she whispered, staring into the flames that were beginning to die down.

"Hey Mattie, do we have anymore wood, or should I drag one of the beach tables out here?" Jerdie said. She looked around. "Mattie?"

"Mattie?" Cookie said standing up.

"Hey Mattie, are you out there?" Tracy yelled toward the water. "Stop scaring us."

"Hang on," Cookie said. "No one goes anywhere," she said as she started sprinting toward the house. She ran into the Great Room and counted. "One, two, three, four. OK, that's good. Still four."

She ran back to the women standing by the fire.

"There's still four glasses," she said running to them. "So she has to be here. She probably wandered off to get a better look at some star like Nostradamus or something. She'll be back. Let's sit here together and wait for her. If we stay together we're safe."

"Unless she's the killer and she's going to get something to kill us with," Tracy said.

"She's not going to kill us," Jerdie said, touching the small handgun in her sweatshirt pocket. "I can guarantee you that."

Cookie looked at Jerdie through the flickering flames, wondering where the new confidence was coming from. She picked up a chair leg with a nail still in it and placed it by her side. "Hey Trace, throw that on the fire, would you? We need to keep the flames going so we can see Mattie coming back from wherever she decided to go. I'm sure she's coming back. There are still four glasses and the glasses don't lie."

III

Tracy, Cookie and Jerdie stared pensively at the bonfire. Occasionally one of them would toss in more wood or palm fronds and the fire would spark and roar. No one said a word. The disappearance of Mattie weighed heavily on their minds. It was the longest they had gone without talking or bickering.

Finally Jerdie spoke."So...I have to tell you something and I don't want you to all freak out."

Cookie and Tracy looked at each other.

"Okay," Cookie said. "Spill."

Jerdie stood up. "After Audrey was killed, I went into my room and opened the drawer on my nightstand. You'll never guess what I found."

The other two women were silent.

Jerdie moved nervously from foot to foot.

"You guys are not going to believe this," she said, putting her hands back into the pocket of her sweatshirt. "Really, it shocked the hell out of me and, you know, we all saw it happen and Audrey said it should happen, so I don't have any clue why it ended up back in my room."

"Are you going to keep babbling, or are you going to tell us what you found?" Cookie said.

"This!" she exclaimed, pulling the pink gun out of her pocket.

Cookie and Tracy both stood up and screamed.

"You're the killer!" yelled Tracy.

"How did you do that, I saw you throw the gun in the ocean!" Cookie cried.

"You're the killer," Tracy yelled again.

Jerdie looked from one vixen to the other.

"No I'm not, I found the gun hours ago and I haven't shot either of you."

"Did you shoot Audrey?" Cookie asked angrily.

"No, I did not shoot Audrey. Did you shoot Audrey?"

Cookie looked confused. "What? No, I don't have a gun. That doesn't make sense. Did you shoot Mattie and hide her body? Is that what's happened? Are you now going to shoot us?"

"I'm not the killer, or I would have already shot you both."

"But how did you get the gun back? Are you sure it's your gun?" Tracy asked.

"How many pink revolvers do you think are on this island?" Jerdie said sarcastically. "I mean, really?"

Tracy sighed heavily. "So does that mean you will put it in the safe with the other items?"

"Are you out of your mind?" Jerdie said. "I threw it in the ocean once, and it came back. I'm keeping it now."

"Or did you hide it somewhere?" Cookie said.

"Are you an idiot? How could I hide it when you all saw it fly into the ocean? I didn't hide it in the ocean, that's not even possible."

"Well, how did you get it back?" Tracy yelled.

"I don't fucking know!"

"Argggh!" screamed Cookie. "And where the hell is Mattie?"

"She's dead," Tracy said glumly.

"Then why haven't we found her body?" Cookie said.

"Maybe someone threw her into the ocean."

"Really, who could throw her into the ocean without us seeing her? How could any of us have had the time to kill her and drag her into the ocean?"

"Well, if she was thrown into the ocean, she's bound to wash back up. Like Jerdie's gun I suppose."

"I don't know," Jerdie said ignoring the dig. "I feel like somebody's watching us, so it could very well be Mattie. "

"But let's get back to the gun," said Cookie. "Why would anyone bring a copy of your gun—or, for the sake of no other reasonable explanation, because nothing is reasonable on this island, why would someone retrieve it from the ocean?"

Jerdie raised her shoulders. "I dunno. It's crazy. What's the point of giving me my gun back?"

"Well if you don't want the gun, you should put it in the safe."

"Not gonna happen."

"Why not?"

"Don't be an ass."

"You won't do it?" asked Cookie.

"Nope."

"Then I guess it's reasonable to come to the conclusion that you are U.N. Owen."

Jerdie laughed.

"I don't give a shit what you think. Think about it. If I'm the killer, why didn't I kill all of you after I found the gun?"

"I have no clue," Cookie said. "But lock up the Goddamn gun," Cookie said through clenched teeth.

"No."

"A gun nut and a pacifist walk into a bar…"

"So not appreciated, Tracy," Cookie said, rolling her eyes.

"The gun nut gets wasted, starts bragging about all the guns he has, rambling off a bunch of gun industry jargon about the special equipment he has for it, on and on, while everyone else in the bar rolls their eyes.

"I protect my house, ain't no one getting one over on me," he said. " You're lookin' at a real man right here! That's why I train from 4 to 5 every day after work down at the range."

The bartender asks, "So how does your wife feel about that, all those guns and the range training every day?"

The nut says, "Pfft, who cares? She just watches her stories, plays with the kittens, or whatever the hell she does while I'm out."

Then the bartender turns to the pacifist and asks, "Hey, buddy, do you know this guy? I notice you're never in here at 4 to 5 either. Do you go to the range too?"

The pacifist glares at the bartender, looks away, and whispers under his breath, "Shut the fuck up, dude. That's her husband."

No one laughed.

IV

"I'm going in the house. It's getting cold," Tracy said.

"Wait, Tracy, are you sure you should go inside? I don't want to go in the house." Like, ever. Too many dead vixens. I'm about to lose my shit," Cookie said.

"And that's the other reason I'm going in the house, Tracy said. "I have to poop and I'm not doing it out here. I've lost all respect for myself. I look like hell, I'm a basket case and I am sober. I do not want to poop outside when there are 12 working toilets in the house. If I get killed going to the bathroom, well then the jokes on me."

Jerdie kicked a little sand.

"Go in the house, I don't care. I'm staying out in the open with my gun. No one can sneak up on me out here."

Tracy locked eyes with Cookie. "Be careful with her," she said. "Be very careful."

Tracy turned and walked onto the patio and headed for the house. Cookie turned around quickly and saw Jerdie putting more fuel on the fire.

"We've got to keep this fire going," Jerdie muttered. "Someone is bound to see it. It's a frigging Burning Man fire, that's what it is. How can they not see it? What is wrong with the world? Why isn't anyone looking for us?"

"Calm the hell down, Jerdie. You're the safest one on the island, carrying that little pink gun around."

"That's right," she replied. "And what makes you so sure I won't shoot you?"

"I have no choice but to trust you," Cookie mumbled. "Besides, I think Mattie is hiding. I think she's the killer."

Jerdie looked around into the darkness.

"Seriously, Tracy is right, I think someone is watching us."

"That's just nerves, Cookie. Or at least I think it is."

"So do you feel the creepy eyes on you too?" Jerdie tossed another piece of driftwood onto the fire. Cookie didn't answer.

"Seriously, it's like this show on HBO I saw once where there were a couple of aliens or zombies or something that landed in a tiny town in Kansas. They started judging people and putting them to death for their crimes, kind of like what's happening here."

Cookie raised her eyebrows. "Aliens and zombies? That's your theory? Have you lost your mind?"

"Pretty much," Jerdie replied with a sick grin. "But it seems that the stupid nursery rhyme is the blueprint for these murders. 'Four little Vixens floating on the sea; A shark swallowed one and then there were three.'"

"Mattie's not here, she got eaten by a shark in the water. Or a land shark."

Jerdie laughed. "Land shark?"

Cookie eyed her suspiciously. "What's so funny?"

Jerdie smirked. "Of course you don't know. Google it. Oh, wait, never mind. I guess you'll never know."

"Whatever, you crazy bitch. But, I'm sure she's dead. Or she's the killer. Or, you're the killer. Or maybe I'm the killer and I don't even know it. God, I would sell my own child for a Xanax."

"Anyhoo, it's Mattie alright. She came out here in advance, set all this up and found a place to hide."

"I don't see how. She's smart, but you know, kind of crazy-smart. It could be her, but I don't know anything anymore."

"That, my dear vixen, is called a conscience." Jerdie paused. "So did you switch the locks at the pageant and cause that girl to drown?" she asked quietly.

"I didn't, the judge said I didn't! Stop accusing me!"

Jerdie laughed. "So you did kill her. Wow, you really wanted to win that title."

Cookie slumped to the ground. A sudden weariness took hold of her body. She filled her hand with sand and let it slip through her fingers.

"Yes, I really wanted to win that crown," Cookie said softly.

"Thanks for admitting it."

Cookie stood up quickly. "What was that? An earthquake?"

"I don't think so, but I felt it too. It was a big thud. And I think I heard someone yell."

They both looked up at the house. The sun was just coming up and the palm trees threw shadows onto the house.

"It came from there. We better go see if it was Mattie or Tracy."

"I can't go, Jerdie. What if it's Tracy?"

"I'm going, I have to know what's happening."

"Fine, I'll come with you," a shaken Cookie said.

They walked past the pool, which was full of empty wine bottles, trash and broken furniture. They hesitated as they came into the kitchen. They didn't find anyone in the kitchen so they wandered around, avoiding the vixen glasses in the Great Room. They slowly ascended the staircase.

They found Tracy at the top of the stairs. She was spread eagle on the marble floor, her head pounded in by a white sandstone statue, which was beside her crushed skull.

Cookie gasped.

"That's from my room," she said, tears rolling down her face as her voice shook. "It was a statue of Dionysus, the God of wine and partying. I was going to sneak it into my suitcase."

Jerdie grabbed Cookie's arm. "That settles it. Mattie is here. She's hiding and we have to find her or she'll take us both out. She can't win, we can't let her get us. I am not dying in a fucking Club Med!"

CHAPTER TWENTY ONE

Laverne—Dead
Justine—Dead
Jill—Dead
Sandra—Dead
Belinda—Dead
Audrey—Dead
Tracy—Dead

October 15

I

The two vixens spent the rest of the day on the sand with the mirrors, taking turns flashing them and following the sun. There were no signs of a plane or a boat. No answering signals. The sky was an incredible color of blue, with only a few perfectly formed clouds floating by. They spent hours, side-by side, not speaking, only flashing the mirrors and sitting in the sand.

Cookie looked up at the house from the beach and finally spoke.

"It's Mattie alright. She's smarter than I ever gave her credit for."

"She's crazy," Jerdie said, taking the gun out of her pocket. "She hid it well. She's twice as smart as we are so we have to be extra careful."

Cookie stared at the gun.

"Can you put that away please? I really hate guns."

Jerdie stared at Cookie for a moment and placed the gun back in her pocket. "Sure thing, I wouldn't want to cause you any stress."

II

"What are we going to do when it gets dark?" Cookie said as they continued to work the mirrors. "We've pretty much used up all the wood we can break without an axe. I don't think we have much left for any kind of fire. We'll be in the dark. I am seriously afraid." Cookie started to cry.

"The weather looks to be OK and there's going to be a full moon tonight. We'll sit out here in the open with our backs to the ocean. I doubt Mattie will sneak up on us on a surfboard," Jerdie said.

"That's true," Cookie said, wiping her eyes. "Let's walk around. I'm freaking out and I can't just sit here like a target."

The bright sunlight reflected off the glassy ocean waves, which cast dazzling flashes of light resembling diamonds in the sea.

"Too bad we can't go swimming," Jerdie said with a nervous laugh as they approached a cluster of large rocks. Then she stopped.

"What's that over there? You see it, by that big rock?"

Cookie stared. "It looks like a bunch of clothes. Did someone throw their clothes in the ocean too?"

"Maybe its seaweed," Jerdie said. "Let's get closer." She reached out her hand and Cookie took it.

"It is clothes!" Jerdie said as they drew closer. "A bunch of them. And a flip-flop. Come on, hustle up, I want to see whose clothes they belong too."

They scrambled over the rocks.

Cookie stopped.

"It's not clothes…it's a person…"

The body was wedged between two rocks, broken and bloated.

The two vixens reached it at the same time. They bent down to the bloated body and turned it over.

"Holy shit, it's Mattie!" Cookie yelled.

CHAPTER TWENTY TWO

Laverne—Dead
Justine—Dead
Jill—Dead
Sandra—Dead
Belinda—Dead
Audrey—Dead
Tracy—Dead
Mattie—Dead

I

Time passed before Cookie's eyes. One more vixen. She had known Mattie for almost 30 years. They played golf together and they went on ski trips to Lake Tahoe. Cookie saw flashes of laughing on camping trips, drinking schnapps on the ski lift and Mattie's disappointed face when she betrayed her.

Jerdie was silent. All she could think about was the time she and Mattie went tobogganing at her mom's cabin. They were drunk and rolled and laughed down the hill, covered in snow. They made snow angels and talked about all the things they loved doing for fun. That's when they were besties, before the stupid women started to get together and everything soured.

Slowly, Cookie and Jerdie lifted their heads and locked eyes.

Jerdie smiled.

"So, this is it Cookie. Just you and me."

Cookie looked nervously down at the body and back to Jerdie.

"It looks that way," she whispered.

"So you know where we stand, right? One of us is the murderer."

"How did you kill Tracy? I'd like to know that," Cookie asked. "I mean, you were with me, so I don't get it."

Jerdie shrugged. "How should I know? I was going to ask you how you could be so heartless as to kill your best friend. Or Miss

Kansas."

"At least, I didn't kill my own sister."

"You don't have a sister, Cookie."

Their eyes met again.

"Why didn't I see it before?" Cookie asked. "You are pure evil. I can see it in your eyes."

"This is it, you understand that, right?" Jerdie spat. "We've come to the end of the line. We're the only ones left and only one of us can be left standing."

"I understand," Cookie replied. She stared out to the horizon. Her home and her family were on the other side of the world and she felt lost. She looked down at Mattie and realized that she had been lost to her years earlier.

"Poor Mattie," she said.

"What, you kill her and now you're sorry? A little late, don't you think?

"Don't you have any pity for her? She's all tangled up with seaweed. We can't leave her like this. We have to take her back to the house. She deserves that much."

"To join the other dead vixens? All nice and tidy, just like you like it? You are one OCD crazy bitch."

"Can we at least get her out of the water? She's so bloated."

Jerdie laughed. "Sure, whatever. We wouldn't want a bloated vixen to be found. We have standards."

Jerdie bent down, tugging at Mattie's body. Cookie leaned against her, helping to pull. She pulled and tugged.

"Damn, she's heavy," Jerdie said.

Somehow, they managed to drag Mattie up the beach, away from the tide.

"You happy now?" Jerdie asked, standing up and wiping the sand off her hands.

"I am indeed," Cookie said.

Her tone bothered Jerdie. Her eyes widened as she put her hand in her sweatshirt pocket. It was, as she had guessed, empty.

She moved back a step and Cookie held up the gun in her hand.

"You bitch. I should have known that you only think about yourself. You could care less if Mattie floats out to sea."

Cookie just stared. She held the gun firmly and pointed it at Jerdie.

"Give me the gun, Cookie," she said through gritted teeth. "Just give me back my fucking gun."

Cookie laughed. "Come and get it," she said.

Jerdie thought quickly. She was tough and street smart. She didn't know if she should stall Cookie and jump her, or try and talk her into throwing the gun back into the sea.

All her life Jerdie had taken risks and they'd paid off. Sometimes she had to walk over others, but dammit, she had to look out for herself. She didn't need anyone to take care of her because she was the smartest, toughest women in the room at all times.

"Come on Cookie, let's be reasonable,"

And then she gracefully leapt across the sand. Cookie pulled the trigger and caught Jerdie in mid-air, a look of surprise frozen on her face as she crashed down onto the beach.

Cookie walked cautiously to Jerdie, but she knew she didn't need to be afraid. She was an excellent shot. She went on hunting trips with Kurt to Colorado every few years. She had purposely shot Jerdie through the heart and she was dead.

II

Cookie sat down on the sand, relief washing over her. It was over at last. There would be no more fear and no more anxiety attacks. She let out a breath and filled her lungs with the salty air and let it out again. She got to her feet and gazed up at the house.

She was alone on the island.

Alone with nine dead vixens.

But hell, she was alive and that's what mattered. She raised her face to the sun and drank in the warmth.

"It's good to be alive," she said, shouting up at the sky.

III

The sun was beginning to descend as Cookie began to walk off the beach, the gun still in her hand. She had stood at the water's edge for what seemed like hours. She was content and happy. She realized that she was hungry and tired. So damn tired. She wanted to take off her clothes and crawl into bed and sleep for days. Maybe tomorrow they would come rescue her. She was supposed to have called home yesterday, so Kurt would start to worry and send someone to look for her soon. Maybe he would even fly out and rent a boat. He could take his time though, she didn't mind staying here. Maybe she would clean up the pool and take a dip. Now that she was alone, she could do anything she wanted. Oh good God, she didn't realize how peaceful it was without all those women fighting and bickering.

She stepped into the house and stopped for a moment. She thought she might be afraid, but she only felt free. Free from fear—this was a good thing, she decided.

It was over. She had won. She had finally taken first place. She had beaten them all with her smarts and had bravely taken out her would-be-killer. Damn, she realized again how drained she was; her body ached. Her eyes were tired and she had lost her sunglasses. Man, she just wanted to sleep.

She smiled to herself.

"I must be brave, sleeping in a house with dead people," she said, laughing to herself.

"I think I'm hungry. Do you want something to eat, Cookie? Sure what do we have?"

Cookie looked in the pantry. "Devon and Two-Buck Chuck. I think I'll pass."

She turned and walked into the Great Room. There were still three vixen wine glasses on the bar.

She laughed.

"You're a little out of the loop, my dear," she said.

Cookie smashed two glasses with her fist. She wrenched the remaining glass from the table, the stem still firmly in place.

"You can hang out with me. We won. We beat them all, just like I knew we would."

The hall was growing dim and she cupped the glass with her bleeding hand and climbed the stairs. Damn, she was growing more exhausted by the minute.

"One little vixen, left all alone. How did it end again? Oh right, she was left all alone because she was the prettiest and the smartest. And then there were none."

Hmm, was that how it went?

At the top of the stairs she stepped over Tracy. Cookie let go of the gun and it bounced off the marble as she held the glass tighter and shuffled down the hallway.

Boy, it sure was quite. Almost too quiet...

"One little vixen left all alone...what was that last line again? Something about winning, or was it something else?

She walked into her room and slowly opened her door...she gave a small yelp.

What was that, hanging from the hook in the ceiling? A noose made with what looked like a pageant sash. And a chair to stand on, a chair that could be kicked away...

That's what she deserved...

And of course, that was the last line of that fucking poem.

"She went and hanged herself and then there were none..."

The last of the vixen stemware fell from her hand and shattered on the teak floor.

Automatically she moved forward. This was the end, she knew it now. This is what Heather felt when she realized Cookie had switched the lock.

"So sleepy. The memories and the nightmares and anxiety attacks never end." She ran her hand through her tangled hair. "I just wanted to win. Oh mommy, you're so mean. I am pretty. I am."

Cookie climbed up on the chair, her eyes unblinking as if she were sleepwalking. She adjusted the silky noose around her neck and stared out the window into the endless horizon. Something caught her eye and she turned. For a moment, she thought she saw Heather, her crown perched on her head, standing in the corner to make sure she did what she had to do.

Cookie kicked away the chair.

Epilogue

One year later

Kurt Armstrong made his way to the front door, trying to avoid knocking a stack of moving boxes onto the floor of the foyer. He was ready to get the show on the road, and move out of the monstrous house that Cookie had insisted they buy 12 years earlier overlooking the ocean. God he hated this house, with its six bedrooms and five bathrooms constructed with bare concrete walls and concrete floors, stainless steel doors and aluminum siding. He felt like he was living in a parking garage. It was a cold house, much like his deceased wife. He couldn't wait to move to his recently purchased Craftsman house off State Street, within walking distance from the beach and downtown with his fiancée, Holly. Thank God for Holly, coming into his life when the media was camped on his doorstep wanting to pry into his business with the suicidal 'Vixen of Vanishing Island.' Between the FBI and the Australian National Police practically ransacking his home and at some point trying to portray him as the mastermind behind 10 deaths on the Australian island, he had been going nuts. He hid out in a retreat in Ojai where the Beatles had laid low for a few months, surrounded by pepper trees, green hills, wildflowers, no booze and lots of quiet. Holly was a yoga teacher at the retreat. With her curly strawberry blond hair, her curves and her beatific smile, he felt like he had been given a second chance at life. Cookie's death had of course shaken him to the core, and he and their two sons had mourned her, but he quickly recognized that the Cookie, who died on the island, was not the Cookie he fell in love with in college. He realized that the more money he made, the more unfeeling and shallow his wife became. He mourned the young Cookie, but not the middle-aged, plastic, status-seeking woman she had become. She had been bringing him down and he vowed to find himself. He lost 20 pounds, threw away his hairpiece and started running to relieve the stress. He was tall and still good-looking in rugged way, and women did sly double-takes when he walked in for mediation.

He had, of course, wanted to find out what had happened to his wife and her friends, longing for the resolution that would put to rest the nugget of guilt that he was feeling with his upcoming nuptials. His sons deserved to know what happened to their mother and find some closure.

He'd quickly become fed up with the cops and the circus of officials trying to solve the case. After six months, he hired a private investigator to look into the deaths of Cookie and the nine other vixens.

Thomas Manning, the P.I., was now at his door. The squat and handsome PI with a full head of grey hair looked the opposite of Kurt as he stood with a notebook in his hand. Kurt ushered him inside.

II

"Ten women dead on an island with no suspects. It doesn't make sense. This case should have been solved months ago," Kurt said as the investigator sat on the low red leather couch.

"By the FBI's own numbers, homicide today is 64 percent. Fifty years ago, it was more than 90 percent," Thomas Manning said. "The cops are under the assumption that there is no perfect crime, and that every contact leaves a trace. Therefore, every crime can, in theory, be solved. But, it's not happening in this case. Too many suspects, too many deaths and too much damn DNA all over the place."

"So the causes of death are the same as in the police report?"

Manning consulted his phone. "Yes, Laverne died of oleander poisoning, Justine died of an overdose of Chloral hydrate and she was smothered. Mattie died by a blow to the head and drowned, Sandra was stabbed in the back, Tracy's skull was crushed, Jill died from a blow to the back of her head, Belinda was injected with poisoned Botox, Audrey and Jerdie were shot and of course you know your wife hung herself."

Kurt winced. Cookie must have gone insane if she actually did kill herself. It was hard to believe, but there didn't seem to be any other explanation.

"Jesus, so the FBI and the Australian cops are stumped? Somebody must know something. How about the helicopter pilot who flew the women onto the island?"

"Josh Benton? Dead," Manning said. "His copter crashed the night after he delivered the last woman to the island. Nothing suspicious at the time, but they're looking into it again."

"And who owned the island? Who made the arrangements?"

"Guy by the name of Jonny Alvarado owns the island. He was in prison at the time of the murders. Still in prison for murder and drug smuggling. Really rich guy, but a nasty piece of work. He'd been trying to sell the island and there are some offers now that it has a history. Some people want to live in a haunted house. This is a haunted island. Go figure. Anyway, so far there's no connection between him and any of the women."

"There's gotta be a financial angle somewhere. Money had to be transferred or...something. Jesus, a ghost didn't kill 10 people," Kurt said.

"Alvarado's job is to launder money, so there's almost no way we can see if anyone paid him. Might have been a favor for someone who hated those women. The pilot did tell a lot of people he was working for someone who was filming a reality show, but that's the story everyone believed."

Kurt kicked a box with his foot and what sounded like china toppled onto the floor.

"Goddamn it, I want an answer. Just one! How in the hell were ten women murdered and no one noticed a thing? The island was a fucking mess when I arrived. Dead bodies, the pool full of trash, half-burned furniture piled high and women's clothing everywhere," he yelled, falling back into a chair.

Manning shrugged. "No one thought anything was off until the authorities came out. The previous owner was Billy Vapid, the punk-rock star. He threw some outrageous parties on that place for more than a decade. The locals got used to taking some wild people out to the rock. It's 20 miles from Sydney, so it's tough to see anything. A couple of Boy Scouts noticed some smoke and someone called in seeing some flashes of light, but other than that, no one saw a damn thing."

Kurt had been the one who sounded the alarm bells. Cookie was supposed to have been home three days earlier and he hadn't heard a word from her. He called the Australian Federal Police, and after finally throwing his weight around and mentioning numerous times that he was a lawyer, he got on the line with detective sergeant Callie Diamond, who called Marine Rescue NSW, who dispatched a boat to the island. When he took the call eight hours later, he was shocked, then devastated. The Aussie papers had a field day accusing his wife, the only one who killed herself, of murdering the others, but no one could prove it. No one could prove anything, for that matter.

"No one reported seeing any boats coming from the island or any aircraft near the time your wife died, so it seems impossible that anyone could have left the island before the rescue boat arrived."

"How about the iPod they found with the voice accusing all of the women of killing someone? Could they figure out whose voice it was?"

"No, it didn't belong to any of the vixens according to the FBI. They used voice analysis and came up with the deduction that it is an unknown female speaker of Indian origin. As in Calcutta, India."

"You mean, it was outsourced?"

"Looks like it," Manning replied, holding in a smile.

"What about the accusations? They were pretty harsh. As for Cookie, she always insisted Miss Kansas's death was an accident."

He cleared his throat.

"I've investigated the accusations against the vixens as best I could, starting with Ms. Allen, who looked to be the first to arrive. That woman did indeed kill her husband's mistress, but she got off with a temporary insanity plea. She completely lost it when her husband dumped her. Said she didn't remember running over her with a grape harvester. She must have had a great lawyer, because that defense hardly ever works. She got a few months in a mental hospital, but after that, she was free and clear.

Then there's Audrey Walsh, she was a host of one of those real-life murder shows on TV. She was famous for surprising a suspect who used his girlfriend as an alibi. He killed himself off camera after she showed him evidence accusing him for his wife's murder. They tried to blame Audrey, but it didn't go anywhere. Her popularity took off after the suicide."

"I know all about Audrey," Kurt said. "She and my wife used to be close. Cookie watched her show every Friday night."

Manning continued to read his notes. "Justine, who was a professional golfer, accidentally killed another golfer by throwing her club in anger. She got off with involuntary manslaughter. Belinda was a suspect in her former business partner's death, but just last week an employee confessed to killing him after he was fired. The woman who jumped to her death off the Golden Gate Bridge did so because the convent threw her out after Sandra told the nuns about her pregnancy. All these accusations this Una person tossed out were cases that the courts couldn't touch, or they found them not guilty on a technicality."

Manning looked at Kurt, adjusted his glasses and continued to read.

"Tracy took the place of a comic who disappeared from the Rio. Cops think he was screwing with the casino and they found out about it. He's probably buried in the desert somewhere. Laverne accidently killed a man who stepped in front of her car. Vegas PD surmised that he did it on purpose. She wasn't cited. Mattie was with her boyfriend when his appendix burst on a camping trip. She was a veterinarian, and she did everything she could to help him, but he died before help arrived. Jerdie's twin sister died of an overdose of heroin, but she died here in the States, and Jerdie lives in Sydney. Of course, you know your wife was charged with involuntary manslaughter for the death of her roommate Miss Kansas. Did she ever tell you what happened with the lock and the water tank?"

"She always claimed it was an accident. Apparently Miss Kansas left her locks at the hotel, and Cookie volunteered to run back to the hotel to fetch the trick lock. She grabbed the first one she saw, which unfortunately turned out to be Heather's gym lock. By the time they broke through the shatterproof glass, she had drowned. Cookie carried that guilt around for the rest of her life. She always acted as if it didn't bother her, but I know it did. Why else would she kill herself?"

"Actually, it doesn't look like she did kill herself."

Kurt jumped up from his chair.

"What the hell are you saying?"

"I'm saying someone using the name U.N. Owen methodically executed 10 women and somehow escaped off the island and into thin air."

"But that's impossible, from what the FBI told me."

"Exactly. From what I've learned, the only possible explanation is that the killer was actually one of the vixens."

"Jesus Christ," Kurt said.

"There wasn't any Wi-Fi on the island, but a few of the women took notes and wrote down some thoughts on their IPhones. Some accused the others. Mattie was very afraid and wrote down some pretty sad stuff, and Tracy jotted down some jokes."

Kurt laughed. "A joker until the end, that was Tracy," he said.

"Jerdie wrote on her phone that "Mattie disappeared," which throws the suspicion on her, but the coroner arrived on the island early on the morning on October 20th and said that all of the women had been dead at least 72 hours and probably longer. He was however very definite about Mattie and that she had been in the water about 10 hours before her body washed up on the beach. This means Mattie must have gone into the ocean sometime during the night of the 14th or the 15th. We know this because we figured out where her body washed up, where it was wedged between two rocks and there were traces of her hair and cloth and blood on them. Now, you could say that she managed to kill the remaining three before she went into the ocean, but that doesn't work either. Mattie's body had been dragged above the high-water mark. We found it way above the reach of any tide. And she was laid out straight on the ground very carefully.

"So someone was still alive on the island after Mattie died?"

"Yes. That leaves Jerdie, Tracy and Cookie. Jerdie was shot, her body was found down on the beach, near Mattie's, and Tracy's body was in the hall with her head crushed by a statue. Cookie of course— well, you know.

"Yes, I know."

"Let's take these deaths one-by-one. First Jerdie. Let's say she smashed the statue on unsuspecting Tracy's head and then she somehow drugged Cookie and strung her up,"

Kurt winced.

"And then she went to the beach and shot herself."

"But who took the gun away from her? I saw in the report that the gun was found up in Audrey's room. Whose fingerprints were on the gun?"

Manning paused. "Cookies'."

"Damn," Kurt said, covering his face with his hands.

"Hear me out. The cops thought that Cookie shot Audrey and then a day later shot Jerdie, took the gun back to the house, crushed her friend Tracy's skull in and then hanged herself. And they liked that theory except it didn't stand up to scrutiny. There's a chair in Cookie's bedroom and on the seat there was a crown, like you would wear if you were in a beauty contest. But she needed that lone chair to climb up, adjust the rope—made out of silk, by the way—around her neck and kick away the chair to finish herself off. Oddly, the chair wasn't kicked over. It was across the room and by a wall with the crown sitting neatly on the chair. Someone else had to have done that."

"That leaves us with Tracy," Kurt said. "I can't even fathom that she could hang Cookie and shoot Jerdie and then smash her own damn head in. You can't commit suicide like that and Tracy wasn't that way. She didn't have a mean bone in her body."

"I agree. Which indicates someone else was on the island. Someone who made the little adjustments to make it look like one of the other women was the killer. But, where would they hide? I mean, other than a few trees and bushes and the house, the island is a big, bare white rock. You can see from almost every vantage point if there was another person around. The cops are certain no one left the island before the rescue boat arrived because there were no other footprints, DNA or fingerprints. So in that case…"

"In that case…?"

Manning sighed. He shook his head and stared at Kurt.

"I'm sorry man, I have no idea who killed them."

Four years after the murders;

A letter in a bottle delivered by the captain of the fishing trawler, 'Anarmandaleg' to the Australian Federal Police:

Dear World:

Ever since I was a little girl, I realized that I was different, a loner pretending to be an extrovert. My greatest pleasures were reading Nancy Drew mysteries and watching horror films such as 'The Omen' and 'Hush, Hush Sweet Charlotte.' I even identified with sweet little Rhonda in the movie, 'The Bad Seed.' I loved old movies and books, and that's why I decided to write my confession on paper with a pen and put it in the wine bottle and throw it into the waves. There's probably a very slim chance that this will be found, but if it does, an unsolved murder mystery (I have high hopes that I've outsmarted everyone) will be explained. Let's start with my very vivid imagination, where I realized that I was very good at building castles of imaginative delusion. This is not something I am ashamed of. In A Midsummer Night's Dream, Shakespeare suggested a link between madness and artistic creativity; 'The lunatic, the lover, and the poet', he wrote, 'Are of imagination all compact.'

I fear, as I morphed into a creative genius, that I've become all three.

Besides those traits, I have a strong sense of morality and justice. I hate to see anyone hurt, either physically or mentally. When I do, I find a way to right the wrong. Especially if I am the one who was wronged.

As Robert Kennedy once said, "Don't get mad, get even."

I think a physiologist would agree, that with my mental constitution being what it was, that being on TV satisfied nearly all of my natural instincts.

Crime and punishment has always fascinated me. I even read True Crime magazines as a child.

Twenty years later, I was thrilled to find a classmate who made fun of me murdered by his wife in a most unusual way featured in the pages of the December, 1980 issue of True Detective in full, gory color. It was a few years later when I was able to publish a story in True Crime that I knew I had found my calling. The story was an actual crime of passion between a man and his lover involving a knife and a bathtub, but I always day-dreamed about even more creative ways of carrying out a murder.

When I first met the vixens, they were young and a few of them were mean and catty. They hurt my feelings, but I didn't want them to know how they hurt me. Over time, I gained their trust and friendship—some more than others—but they always went back to their true personalities. It wasn't only me that they begrudged, as I knew they were jealous of my intelligence, my wit and even my beauty. Other innocent people stood in their way of fame or success, so they found ways to hurt them and even get rid of them. I took no pleasure in seeing them hurt others, but I developed a thick skin over the years. I have the reputation as cold and calculating in my personal life as well as my career, but nothing could be farther from the truth.

Over the years, as I spent more and more time with the vixens I felt as if I was being pulled into their web of gossip and backstabbing. I couldn't leave. It was like passing a car accident and willing myself not to look—but of course I would always look.

As they turned on each other and their claws and barbs grew sharper, I could only think of serving justice. I had to walk away because I wanted to literally kill them at the monthly luncheons. I dreamt separately of pushing one of them in front of a truck, or running them over with the boat while they were skiing on the lake. I wanted to drug their martinis and push them out into the snow on ski trips and I prayed for them to crash their jets into a mountaintop.

As I grew famous, I knew I wanted something bold, something that would make great TV. I wanted to win sweeps week with my own crime.

I needed to kill. The vixens pushed me to want to kill them. Every single one of them.

But of course, I still have my senses—I'm not a total psychopath.

Then the idea came to me! Each of the vixens (God, how I hated that stupid moniker, but I needed to call them something catchy) had, in some way, caused a death or harmed someone, gravely, either intentionally or by accident. (Although, I do believe there are no accidents.)

That was the beginning of my idea to not commit just one murder, but to make a big bang, to kill a group of women that the public would eventually see deserved to die. I began to create my murder plan.

During the last few years I have been seeing a psychiatrist because I am smart enough to realize that I was having acute symptoms of psychosis because of the influence of the hallucinations and delusions on my thinking. Oh yes, I am very, very smart and I can admit to my own shortcomings—unlike some people.

But oh, those anti-psychotic meds. How I hated them! They interfered with my social and sex life. I couldn't deal with the side effects. I included myself in my grand scheme, but I wanted to experience the thrill of the unfolding drama and go out in a blaze of glory and notoriety.

But enough about me—ha-ha—let me tell you how I murdered the vixens on Vanishing Island.

As you might have guessed, Jonny allowed me to use his island. We had a secret affair years and years ago, and he knows of my mental illness. I didn't tell him of my plans, only hinted at a few things, and he was fine with it. I didn't want to implicate him, as he's always the naughty boy and in hot water with the authorities—even in prison. Quite honestly, I will miss his kindness.

I hired the helicopter pilot. Benton was a shady guy, not like Jonny. He smuggled hard drugs, something I don't approve of. He was also responsible for introducing a friend's daughter to meth, and she ended up killing herself at the young age of 19. I sent the pilot a box of chocolate covered macadamia nuts laced with angel dust, which I had delivered the day after he brought the last vixen to the island. I can only guess that he crashed his helicopter. That works for me.

The order of the deaths of the vixens was well thought out. There were, among the women, varying degrees of crimes and guilt. Those whose crimes were the lightest, I decided, should die first and not suffer the stress and fear that the more cold-blooded vixens were going to suffer, although I have to admit, I started with Laverne because quite honestly, she was the most annoying.

When the recording played accusing everyone, I watched their faces and their actions and have no doubt they were all guilty of the crimes that I had accused them of. While they were screaming and yelling at each other, I managed to slip a powder made from oleander into Laverne's drink. No one noticed and no one suspected anything at the time.

Justine met her death painlessly, although her face bruised when I put the pillow over it. Who knew that would happen? I put a roofie in her wine and she was already asleep when I smothered her with the pillow.

We all searched the island after that in a panic to find the killer and a way to escape, but we realized there were just the eight of us vixens. Everyone was accusing each other and it was like the Ultimate Survivor TV show. It was pretty damn thrilling to tell you the truth, and I only wished that it was being filmed. Jill was an easy mark, as she was waiting to be killed. I think she was relieved to see me right before I smashed her head with a huge rock, which I threw into the ocean.

When we all got naked and searched the bedrooms I swear, I would have won an Emmy for that brilliant directing!

I realized I needed an ally and I chose Mattie. She was smart, although seriously strange, but very gullible. All her suspicions were for some reason directed at Jerdie and I pretended to agree with her. I told her I had an idea that would trap the murdering vixen into showing herself.

I killed Sandra in the early morning. She was making her Holy Granola and had her headphones on and didn't hear me approach. I stabbed her and I have to say I didn't find any pleasure from it. Too messy.

I slipped Belinda a slow acting allergy pill, the kind that makes you tired, and by the time she had run a few miles, and sat down to rest, she was a little ditzy. The bumblebee/Botox thing was somewhat silly, but it made me happy. I mean, who the hell brings Botox on vacation?

It was then that I told Mattie that we had to trick the others into thinking I was dead, that way the real murderer would flip out. If I pretended to be dead, I could sneak around the house and watch everyone and the only person watching me would be Mattie.

With the help of a makeup kit from work and using FX wax and latex blood, I made my face to look like I had been shot. Mattie pronounced me "dead."

After they carried me to my room, I was free to skulk around the property. I was, in a sense, a ghost.

I had made a time to meet Mattie at midnight—mainly because it was when Nancy Drew always met with the killer—and we met on her balcony. It was on the backside of the house, over a cropping of sharp rocks. She wasn't the least bit suspicious of me, which was her biggest mistake. If only she had remembered the words of the poem "SHARK…"

It was easier than I thought. I said, "Holy shit, is that a boat down by the rocks?" She leaned over the rail and a quick push sent her off balance and into the ocean below. It's a good thing she hit the rocks, because she was a hell of a swimmer.

I forgot to tell you about the gun! Luckily, Jerdie posted photos of her gun on Facebook—God, I love Facebook! I bought an exact copy of the gun, so when we tossed her gun in the ocean, I had another one. I snuck back into her room and put the copy in her drawer. I wish I could have seen the look on her face when she saw the second gun! Oh well, I was having more than enough fun to entertain me in my last hours.

Now it really got good. I had three remaining vixens, so afraid of each other I wished I could go to commercial and savor the scene. I watched them from the window of the house. When Tracy came inside, I had the statue—I felt a little bad about that one—I always liked her jokes—and smashed her in the back of the head.

Eventually, from the window I saw Cookie shoot Jerdie. I knew she would do it. She's an Alpha dog like me. That's why we got along and why we butted heads.

Anyway, as soon as she shot her, I set the stage in her bedroom.

I wasn't sure it would work, but I knew she was so stressed and alone. She hated being alone. I hoped that her physiological state was such a mess and the suggestion of the poem would send her over the edge. And it did. She hanged herself before my very eyes as I stood in the closet looking through the crack.

After that, I picked up the chair and set it against the wall. The crown was my last dig at her. I love having the last word.

And now?

I'll finish writing this letter, put it in a bottle and throw it as far as I can into the ocean.

Why?

Well, I thought I explained it rather well.

It was my idea to invent a murder mystery that no one could solve. Of course, the recognition and the notoriety is something I won't be able to see, but I know it will come. TV shows will be produced, Wikipedia pages will be written and ghoulish fan clubs will take root.

I just hope this damn bottle finds its way into the hands of the authorities sooner than later.

So, that about wraps it up. As soon as I finish writing this I will go into my room and lay down on my bed. To my reading glasses is attached what seems like a thin black cord, but it's really an elastic cord. I will lay the weight of my body on the glasses. I will loop the cord around the door handle and attach it, not too solidly, to the gun. What I hope will happen is this:

My hand, protected with a hankie, will press the trigger. My hand will fall to my side, the gun, pulled by the elastic will recoil to the door, jarred by the door handle it will detach itself from the elastic and fall. The elastic, released, will hang down innocently from my glasses on which my body is lying. A hankie on the floor won't be suspicious.

I will be found on my bed, shot through the forehead, just like everyone thought. Times of death will be messed up since we don't know when we will be found. Either way, I am dead.

When the rescuers arrive, they will find 10 dead vixens and a mystery on Vanishing Island.

Love and kisses,
Audrey Walsh.

Acknowledgments

For the encouragement of my wonderful friend and long-distance writing partner, Kathleen Mallery Buckstaff, I thank the Universe and Lindsay Mead McCrea for the introduction. This novel could not have been written without Kathleen's encouraging texts, (cheerleader-style as in, "Go team!) emails, stickers and weekly phone calls.

As luck would have it, I met my editor (and dream maker), Morgan Fraser, in the tiny town of Chelan, WA. Her love of travel and her bravery surpasses all. She is also an honest writer and an inspiration to many. Another shout-out to the Universe.

I thank my non-vixen friends for loving me for who I am and not rolling your eyes at my crazy ideas in life-style and career choice.

I thank my parents for allowing me to be creative and I thank my sisters for having my back.

I want to thank my aunt and uncle, Jacqueline and Rik Jeans, for giving me a quiet place in the forest to write. If we hadn't had so many 'happy hours' on the deck, I might have finished writing this book sooner. I thank my husband, Ralph T. Reed, my daughter, Aja Reed, and my son, Samuel T. Reed, for coming on this adventure and supporting my dreams of making a living as a writer. It's always going to be a hustle, but I couldn't imagine it any other way.

Candice Reed's next beach mystery, SASSY TRASHY, ST. TROPEZ will be published January of 2018.

Made in the USA
San Bernardino, CA
26 June 2017